Table o

Frightfully Dead
A Pumpkin Hollow Mystery
by
Kathleen Suzette

Chapter One

"OH, THAT LOOKS DELIGHTFUL," Linda Reid said, watching me carry a tray of fudge to the display case.

I nodded. "It smells and tastes delightful, too." My mom had outdone herself this year. She was always tweaking recipes, trying to improve on them, and this year for Pumpkin Hollow Days, she had made pumpkin spice fudge, as she always had, but then she made another version of it. This version had a bottom layer of pumpkin spice fudge, and it was topped with a thin layer of caramel. I had nearly eaten myself sick while she made test batches for us to try out. Each batch had been what I considered perfect, but Mom was the ultimate perfectionist, and she wasn't satisfied until the fudge reached the perfect level of spice and sweetness.

Linda was filling candy jars with black and orange jellybeans. "Your mother is so creative with her recipes. I wish I had that kind of creativity."

I shut the display case door. "Me too. I'm afraid all I can do is copy what she's done. I don't know what we're going to do when she retires." It had been on my mind lately that my sister

Christy and I needed to start thinking about how we were going to run the candy store when our mother got tired of the early hours and all the work. Would things run as smoothly as they did now? I hoped so, but I wasn't sure.

Christy came out of the kitchen with a tray of chocolate fudge. "We should have stopped by Amanda's and picked up some coffee. I swear I can hardly keep my eyes open."

I nodded. "Me too. Ethan and I stayed up late watching an old movie last night. I hate when I do that, but that never stops me from doing it."

Linda chuckled. "Just wait until you get to be my age. You'll be in bed nice and early. Trust me."

I shook my head. My goal was to be responsible about going to bed on time so I wouldn't be tired in the morning, but so far, I was like a nine-year-old who refused to go to bed on time. I knew I would pay for it today, and yet I still stayed up.

Mom came out of the kitchen carrying a tray of vanilla marshmallows. "Are we about ready for the day?"

"Just about," Linda said. "The shelves, bulk bins, and canisters are filled, and we are going to have a wonderful Pumpkin Hollow Days."

We had worked hard to change up the décor of the store for Pumpkin Hollow Days, buying a few more decorations and changing out the ones that had been on display for a while. Between me, my mom, and my sister, we had a lot of Halloween decorations, and we didn't have room to keep them all out at once. We added more orange and clear twinkle lights to the interior, as well as more artificial pumpkins and jack-o'-lanterns.

The store looked festive and was as much fun to look at as it was to buy candy from.

I glanced toward the front door at the small crowd already gathering. Pumpkin Hollow Days was about to begin. I took a deep breath, inhaling the scents of chocolate, pumpkin spice, and vanilla. There was nothing else like those scents in the entire world.

"I like your costume. Can I borrow it some time?" Christy was dressed as a vampire, and I wore my Gypsy costume. During Pumpkin Hollow Days, the merchants dressed up. It was one of the most fun parts of the event.

"Sure, if I can borrow your sixties costume."

"You bet."

Linda turned to my mother. "Ann, maybe we should trade costumes some time." She was dressed as a witch, with orange and black striped stockings and a black pointy hat.

My mother laughed. She had dressed as a 1920s flapper. "We sure could. Let me know what you want to borrow."

Somebody knocked impatiently on the door. I smiled. "I guess they want in." The crowd was growing, but it was still ten minutes until opening time.

"Go ahead and open the door," Mom said. "We're about ready anyway."

Christy unlocked the door, holding it open for the customers. Some of them were dressed in Halloween costumes, and some were in their regular clothes. It was fun when the customers dressed up. It added to the Halloween feel of the town.

"I hope you have pumpkin spice fudge," an older lady said as she hurried to the display case and bumped into an elderly man. You had to admire the enthusiasm.

"We certainly do," Mom said. "What would Pumpkin Hollow Days be without pumpkin spice fudge?"

"We have the regular pumpkin spice fudge, and my mother made a caramel pumpkin spice fudge, too." I pointed out the new flavor, and the woman's eyes lit up.

"Now, that does look good." She looked up at me. "I hate to do it, but I think I'm going to need a half pound of each. And four of those big marshmallows and three haystacks." She looked over her shoulder at the other customers sheepishly, but they were all focused on their own candy needs and wants. "That's a lot of candy, I guess."

I shook my head as I got to work on her order. "Pumpkin Hollow Days only comes around once a year. Who can blame you for indulging? I work here five days a week, and believe me, I am indulging far more than I should, but it's all so good I can't help it." Some days my appetite was blind to the candy, but when new items were introduced, it woke up. The smell of fudge being made was too good to pass up.

"If I worked here, it would be a disaster," she said.

I chuckled. "I hope you're going to take in all the attractions today. The haunted farmhouse is one of my favorites."

She nodded. "Oh, mine too. But I'll have to wait until the Halloween season for my favorite attraction."

I looked up from the fudge I had just cut. "Oh? What's that?"

"The corn maze." She grinned. I was a little surprised the corn maze was her favorite attraction. Horror movie characters jumped out at unsuspecting visitors to the corn maze, and it wasn't everyone's cup of tea.

I gasped dramatically. "You sure are daring. That one is too much for me." I didn't care for horror movies, and having someone jump out at me with a chainsaw roaring was not my idea of fun.

She laughed now. "I know, I know. My grandson said I wasn't a normal grandmother when I told him it was my favorite." She shrugged. "I guess you can just call me extra-grandma, then."

I chuckled and put the fudge into a paper bag with pumpkins printed on it. The bags we ordered this year had a fun, retro look to them. "Normal is boring. You keep being extra."

"Oh, I will. I will."

I was excited about Pumpkin Hollow Days. It only lasted two weeks in July, but it was a nice taste of what the Halloween season would be like. Growing up in a Halloween-themed town had been a fun, unique experience. There had been a time when I thought I was done with this place, and I went away to college for far too many years, expecting to never return. But I was wrong, and I was never so glad to be wrong. I don't know what I was thinking back then.

I rang up my customer, and she left. "Hi, Mia, I saw that you opened a few minutes early, and I just had to stop by and get some pumpkin spice fudge," Nina Black said.

"Hi, Nina, we've got a new twist on an old favorite." I pointed to the tray of caramel pumpkin spice fudge. Nina owned the jewelry store in town. She was dressed as Little Orphan Annie, and her red wig was wild this morning.

She inhaled deeply. "You really know how to torture a girl. I had better get a quarter pound of that. Oh, and a quarter pound of the regular pumpkin spice. You know how George is a stickler for everything classic, and if I don't bring him some of the regular, I'll have to come right back."

I laughed. "George does love his routines, and I don't blame him. I love mine, too. It's just that Ethan says I'm too young to have so many of them, and he makes me step out of the box now and then." I was a little worried I might be allowing myself to become complacent in life. I had a job that I loved, a husband I loved even more, and I lived in a cute little cottage that I was also fond of. Not that I was planning on settling into a life without any excitement. I was only thirty-two, and I had a lot of living to do. But sometimes I did feel as if I would never make any changes to my life, and the fact that it was fine with me had me a little worried.

She nodded. "I can't get George to do anything fun anymore. I told him being that way would move him closer to the grave, and Halloween-themed town or not, I wasn't ready to visit him in his grave." She chuckled. "George is the best thing that ever happened to me, but I'd like to go out now and then."

I grinned as I cut and wrapped her fudge. "I hear you. A night out is good for the soul, as well as the marriage." More customers entered the store and excitedly hurried over to the shelves that held chocolate pumpkins, orange and black candy of every variety, white chocolate ghosts, and chocolate witches. We made a lot of the candy that we carried here at The Pumpkin

Hollow Candy Store, but some of it was brought in from other manufacturers.

Nina paid for her fudge and hurried off to open her shop. Pumpkin Hollow Days had been a wonderful addition to the Halloween season. It gave us a chance to show off the town during the summer—a season that before Pumpkin Hollow Days was one of the slowest business seasons of the year.

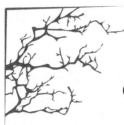

Chapter Two

I TURNED AND LOOKED at Christy after the customers had cleared out. "Not a bad little rush for the first day of Pumpkin Hollow Days."

She nodded and went to the front window, peering out. "Not bad at all. Here comes the parade."

I picked up the two stools behind the counter and hurried over to join her. Mom, Linda, Lisa Anderson, and Carrie Green were all walking in the parade, representing the candy store. Lisa was going off to college in the fall, so this would be her last chance to participate in something like this for the candy store.

"I love a parade," I said, grinning.

Christy snorted and shook her head. "You and show tunes." She reached for some taffy that was wrapped in black and orange waxed paper. "I'm kind of glad we aren't walking in it this year. It's warm out there. This is the perfect place to watch the parade from."

I nodded and took the two pieces of taffy that she offered me. "I don't mind being in it, but it's nice to let the others have a turn."

We watched as first the police cars and fire trucks came down the street, sirens blaring, and then the high school marching band. There was something about a parade that always put me in a good mood, and I couldn't help smiling from ear to ear as we watched the homemade floats, horses, the 4-H club with their animals dressed in costumes, and bands from nearby schools pass by. The sidewalk was lined with tourists, but we still had a good view of the parade. Maybe Christy was right. This was the perfect place to watch the parade from.

Christy tilted her head. "Look at all the little ones in their costumes. They're so cute."

"Oh, here comes Amanda and Isabella." I grabbed some lollipops and ran through the door with them. Amanda was my best friend from high school and her little girl was two now. Amanda had started Isabella at the local daycare, and the daycare kids were dressed up in their Halloween costumes, showing them off as they marched. "Hi, sweet girl," I said and handed Isabella an orange and white striped lollipop. she was dressed as Sleeping Beauty, and she was grinning from ear to ear. In a flash, I made the rounds to all fourteen kids in her group, handed them each a lollipop, grinned at Amanda, and hurried back to the shop.

Christy laughed when I walked through the door, breathing hard. "I think you may have set some kind of record for handing out lollipops."

I breathed out hard. "I may have. Either I need to start exercising regularly, or I need to not run." I inhaled, trying to steady my breathing. Mom and the girls would be tossing candy to the kids sitting on the sidewalk, but the kids walking in the parade might not get any unless someone thinks about giving them some. At least Isabella's group would have the lollipop.

We waved to Mom and the girls when they walked by and watched as the kids on the sidewalks scrambled to pick up the wrapped candy they tossed. This was one of the most enjoyable events of the two weeks. How had I thought I could leave this life behind? I shook my head. I wasn't thinking.

A scream came from outside, and we looked at each other.

"What was that?" Christy asked.

I shook my head slowly. "Maybe it's a part of the parade." Being a Halloween-themed town allowed for a variety of groups to walk in the parade. Some dressed up as monsters or their favorite Halloween character and did short skits when they got in front of the judge's platform. I looked out at the crowd, and while some were looking down the street, no one looked concerned.

"Maybe so," she said.

We watched as the parade wound down, with Jack Skellington dressed as Santa pulling up the rear. Yeah, we mixed our holidays around here. I glanced at the clock. The parade lasted almost two hours, and I was starving for lunch.

Christy turned to me. "I'm hungry."

I laughed and picked up my stool and put it behind the counter. "You're a mind reader. I was thinking the same thing. When Mom and the others get back, we'll be able to take our lunch. I think I want a burger."

She brought her stool around behind the counter. "Sounds good. We can walk to the Haunted Hollow Café if you want."

I nodded and took a deep breath as a lot of the people who had been sitting on the sidewalk watching the parade streamed through the front door. I crossed my fingers that the others wouldn't take too long to get here because we were going to need help.

"Wasn't that a wonderful parade?" a woman holding two children by the hand asked me.

I nodded. "The Halloween parade is the best. I love watching it." I turned to the kids. The girl was dressed as a ballerina, and the boy was dressed as Blue from Blues Clues. "Did you kids like the parade?"

The little girl nodded. "It was so fun! I wish I could be in it!"

The mother looked into the display case. "Maybe we should ask if you can be next year. I think I need half a pound of pumpkin spice fudge, and half a pound of vanilla. Oh, and how about two chocolate pumpkins for the kids?" She darted over to the shelf, weaving in and out of the other customers, and grabbed two foil-covered chocolate pumpkins and brought them back while I cut fudge for her.

A line quickly built up, and Christy and I worked together to wait on everyone, cutting and wrapping fudge and ringing up purchases. Twenty minutes later, Mom and the girls returned, their cheeks pink from being out in the sun. I'd like to say that we had waited on all the customers and cleared them out before they got back, but as soon as we waited on one, it seemed like two more took their place in line.

"Oh, goodness," Mom said breathlessly as she came behind the counter. "Why don't you and Christy take your lunch, and we'll take care of the customers?"

"Are you sure?" I asked. "It's awfully busy."

She nodded. "There are four of us. We'll get the line down, and everyone will get their candy."

"You don't have to tell me twice," Christy said. "I'm starving."

Linda and Mom took over the customer we were helping, and we slipped out the door.

"Wow, we are crazy busy," Christy said. "I'm glad they came back when they did."

We hurried along the sidewalk, doing our best to avoid the tourists. A few blocks down, I breathed in, turning to Christy. "This may be our most crowded Pumpkin Hollow Days yet."

She nodded, but she didn't look at me. "I wonder why those police cars and that ambulance are at the jewelry store?"

I turned to look. I had been preoccupied with walking around tourists, and I wasn't looking very far down the street. I shook my head. "I waited on Nina this morning before the parade. I hope she and George are all right."

We hurried and crossed the street just as they put the empty gurney back into the ambulance. "Whew," Christy said. "Looks like whoever they came for must be all right if the ambulance is getting ready to leave without them."

I nodded, but just as we got to the front door of the jewelry store, my husband Ethan pulled up and double parked next to a police car. "Uh oh." It wasn't that I wasn't glad to see Ethan, but I thought I knew why the ambulance was leaving without a patient.

Ethan looked at me as we approached, his brow furrowed. "What are you two doing here?"

An officer was standing in front of the door, blocking it. "We were walking to lunch. What are you doing here?"

He sighed, stepping closer. "I need to talk to Nina. About her husband." He looked at me meaningfully.

I gasped. "She bought some fudge this morning. George? Really?"

He nodded gravely. "I just got the call. I'm going to talk to her. I'll see you later tonight."

I nodded as he went inside. Through the glass, I could see Nina talking to an officer. She was waving her arms around, and then she crossed them in front of herself, her shoulders shaking.

"Oh, no."

"Poor Nina," Christy said. "Did she say if George was feeling sick?"

I shook my head. "She was picking up some fudge for him. She didn't mention if he wasn't feeling well, but if Ethan was here, I don't think he was sick."

"I guess not."

I looked at Christy. "Maybe we should leave. I don't want to get in the way. I just feel bad for Nina." Ethan was a detective with the police department, and he was only called if there was something terrible that had happened.

She nodded. "We'll stop by and see her in a couple of days and check on her if it's as bad as Ethan thinks it is."

We hurried on to the Haunted Hollow Café, where they had just about the best food in Pumpkin Hollow. If George was murdered, I couldn't imagine who would do it. Unless someone tried to rob the store while the parade was going on. Someone might have thought it was a good time to rob the store with everyone distracted.

Chapter Three

"I HOPE NINA IS OK," Mom said.

We were cleaning up the shop and watching the clock as it slowly made its way to 9:00 pm. We stayed open late during Pumpkin Hollow Days and the Halloween season, and right then I was so tired I could barely keep my eyes open. Mom had gone home and taken a nap, then she came back, worried there wouldn't be enough fudge.

I nodded, wiping the top of the counter. There had been so many sticky fingers that touched it that it was almost opaque in spots. "Me too." We tried to keep it clean between customers, but when there was a line to the door, it didn't happen.

"Have you heard anything from Ethan?" Christy asked with a yawn. "Excuse me."

"Just a text saying George was dead. Hopefully he won't be too late getting home tonight." Christy and I had intended to go home earlier, but things were so busy that we decided to stay all day. Another shift of employees that we had hired as temps had arrived in the afternoon, and they were cleaning up the kitchen now.

Christy came to sit on one of the stools behind the counter. "Everything is re-stocked, ready for tomorrow." She turned to me. "Nina didn't seem upset about anything when she came in?"

I shook my head. "No. She seemed just as happy as she always is when she came in. She bought some fudge and was heading back to her shop to open up." I'd thought about it all day, and I was sure that her husband George had to have been robbed. George was a homebody, and I couldn't imagine him stirring up trouble with anyone.

The bell over the door jingled, and I looked up. I was surprised to see Nina standing there, tears streaked down her face. She was still wearing her costume, and she looked exhausted.

"Did you hear?" She looked from me to Mom and then to Christy.

Mom nodded. "I'm so sorry, Nina. Is there anything we can do to help?" Mom held her arms out to her, and Nina fell into them, sobbing.

"I just don't know who would do this. I can't believe this is happening."

Tears came to my eyes. I hurried over to hug her, and Christy did the same.

"I'm sorry, Nina," I said. "I'm so sorry."

We stood there hugging her for what seemed like forever. When we let her go, I locked the shop door. Christy grabbed a box of tissues beneath the counter and passed it around. We were all in need of them.

"Nina, what happened?" I asked gently. I didn't want to pry, but someone murdering George didn't make any sense.

She sniffed, wiping at her eyes with a tissue. "After I left here, I went back to the shop. The door was unlocked, but the closed sign was in the window, so no one had come in. I locked it when I left, and I just assumed George had unlocked it before I got back and forgotten to turn the sign to open and that he was working in the back like he always does. Of course, customers came right in when I turned the sign to open. People want souvenirs, you know how it is. I was so busy that I didn't even go to the back room to check on him until nearly the end of the parade. That's when I found him." She broke down again, and Mom put an arm around her to steady her.

"What happened to him?" Christy asked, dabbing at her eyes.

"Someone shot him." Her voice broke, and she began sobbing again.

Christy gave me a shocked look as Mom held Nina again. It broke my heart that George was dead and Nina was going through this. Nina was in her early fifties, and George had been ten years older. They had run the jewelry store for more than thirty years.

"I'm so sorry," Mom murmured, patting her back as she held her.

When Nina got ahold of herself, she looked at us. "I was only gone about twenty minutes. I took my time walking over here, looking into the other shop windows. I wasn't gone very long. I don't understand this."

"Do you think someone tried to rob him while you were gone?" I asked.

She shook her head. "There was nothing out of place up front. I've been going over the more expensive jewelry to see if anything was taken, but it's all there. The cash register hadn't been disturbed, so I don't think it was a robbery."

"I'm so sorry this happened," Mom said.

"Ethan will find the killer," I assured her. And Christy and I would also look around and see if we could find out anything, but I didn't say it.

"How was George doing?" Christy asked. "I hadn't seen him for a while."

She sniffed. "He was doing fine. He was talking about maybe selling the shop, but I told him that we needed to wait. He was only sixty-two. If he retired now, I was afraid we would run out of money in our retirement account. Plus, I like running the jewelry store. It's nice to get to visit with the customers, and I enjoy picking out merchandise to sell. It's all I've known for so long that I wouldn't know what to do with myself if we sold it."

I squeezed her shoulder. "I know exactly what you mean. When I went to college, I swore I would never return to Pumpkin Hollow, but the truth is, I thought about home a lot, and I missed the candy store."

She smiled through her tears. "You do get used to doing something like this, don't you? People complain about working in retail, but when it's your own business, it's different."

"It certainly is. And I know George enjoyed what he did. I ran into him at the grocery store a month ago, and we talked for a few minutes. I told him the thought of retiring had crossed my mind a time or two, but I'm not ready. He smiled and said that he didn't know for sure if he was or not," Mom said.

She chuckled. "That was George. He was in such a rut in life that even quitting working was something he had to think about. I kept thinking that one day I'll just know when it's time to retire, but I've got a few years until I can collect social security, so I'm not even entertaining the idea."

"He's going to be missed," Christy said. "The community and the customers will be sad about this."

Nina blew her nose, nodding. "I know. We have so many repeat customers during the Halloween season and Pumpkin Hollow Days. I hate to be the one who has to tell them that he's gone. It won't be the same working there without him, either. I don't know if I can do it, to tell you the truth."

"I know you have a business to run, but don't go back too early," Mom said. "Take some time off, and don't go back until you're ready. Your employees can handle things, can't they?"

She nodded. "Yes, Kelly and Elizabeth can handle things. I might have them close the shop a little earlier in the evening than we planned for Pumpkin Hollow Days so they don't get worn out. But I don't know if they can do it all themselves."

"I can help on one of my days off," Christy said. "That way they can have a day off, too."

"If we both gave you one of our days off, that would make two days Kelly and Elizabeth can take off," I suggested. The idea of working my day off didn't excite me, but I would do it for Nina. I couldn't imagine going through what she was going through now. If I lost Ethan, it would be the end of me.

She smiled. "You girls are too generous, but I couldn't ask you to do that."

"Maybe I can look at our work schedule and send a couple of my girls to work in your shop? I hired some temporary employees, and to tell you the truth, I feel like we have more than enough people to get us through the holiday season."

Nina shook her head. "I couldn't put you out. I know it's busy in here with all the customers. Everyone wants to stop by the candy store when they visit Pumpkin Hollow. And then you have online orders, too."

Mom waved a dismissive hand. "Nonsense. We'll manage. I've got great employees, and they won't mind working over there. It will be fine, I'm sure."

Tears came to Nina's eyes again. "If you're sure. I don't want to put you out, though."

Mom shook her head. "You're not putting me out. Tell Kelly and Elizabeth I'm going to make up a schedule and send my girls over to help. We'll figure out how to have coverage at both stores."

Nina began sobbing and hugged my mom again. "You're the best friend I've ever had. You all are."

"Aw," I said, and Christy and I hugged her again. "If there's anything you need, let us know. We can pick up food for you if you don't feel like cooking or going out to get it. Anything. Just let us know."

She nodded. "I can't believe how kind you all are. I'm going to go home and call the girls and let them know they'll be hearing from you, Ann. I can't thank you all enough."

"You have enough to worry about," Mom said. "You go home and get some rest."

Mom saw her to the door and then locked it after her. She turned around and sighed. "That was good of you girls to offer to help. We'll work on making this work for all of us."

I nodded. I was still in shock that someone had Killed George Black. I couldn't think of one person that had something against him.

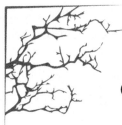

Chapter Four

"OH, MY GOODNESS, THIS looks bad, doesn't it?"

I smiled at the woman at the front counter. She had just emptied her arms of a pile of candy that would make anyone with a sweet tooth drool. She had chocolate pumpkins, white chocolate ghosts, at least a pound of taffy, black and orange jellybeans, and an incredibly large amount of orange and white swirled lollipops.

"Nope. It doesn't look bad at all. There's nothing wrong with indulging in sweets once in a while." I got started ringing her up.

"That's what I tell my husband. And besides, we have three kids. It's not like they won't help me eat it all." She looked into the display case. "Oh my, I'm going to need a pound of pumpkin spice fudge, and half a pound of the caramel pumpkin spice." She sighed, shaking her head. "My husband has the kids down at the pumpkin carving contest, so he can't say I shouldn't buy all of this. He'll thank me later."

I chuckled, and Christy came to cut fudge for her. "It sounds like you know what you're doing. What he doesn't know won't hurt him."

She nodded. "You better believe it."

"This caramel pumpkin spice fudge is delicious," Christy said as she weighed a piece for her.

She nodded. "I don't doubt it. We come here to Pumpkin Hollow every Halloween season and Pumpkin Hollow Days, and everything we've ever bought here has been very good."

I started putting some of the candy into a bag for her. "That's what we like to hear."

"Do you know when the jewelry store is going to be open? I stopped by, but there was a closed sign in the window. My girls and I always get a cute charm bracelet or some other souvenir of our visit."

I smiled. Ethan had said the shop would be closed for a couple of days while he completed his investigation. I opened my mouth to give her an excuse, but Christy beat me to it.

"I heard they had a water leak, and the shop will be closed for a couple of days."

The woman frowned. "Oh, I hate to hear that. We so look forward to getting something each time we visit."

"It's a shame they're closed and missing the first weekend of Pumpkin Hollow Days. If you don't live too far away, maybe you could come back next weekend? I'm sure they'll be open then," I said.

She smiled and nodded. "We're only a little over an hour away. It will give me another excuse to stop in here and get some more candy."

"I like how you think," Christy said.

Sunday was as busy as Saturday was, and while I loved to be busy while at work, it was tiring. Mom had talked to Nina this morning, and she was staying at home for a few days. Her two sons would be arriving for the funeral and other relatives planned to visit her.

"I've got more fudge!" Grace Andrews announced. In one hand, she held a tray of pumpkin spice fudge, and in the other a tray of peanut butter fudge. Grace was in her early forties, and she was one of the ladies Mom had hired as a temp to work through Christmas.

"Just in time. We are out of pumpkin spice fudge," I said. "We've been selling it like crazy." I opened the display case door so she could set the trays inside.

She chuckled. "Your mom and Linda are working their fingers off, making fudge back there. The kitchen smells delightful. You really should think about making candles in the scent of your mom's fudge."

I turned to her. "Oh my gosh, don't get me started on candles. I love them. Fudge scented candles would be awesome." This was the first year that Grace was working for us, and I liked her. She was always happy and full of energy. Today she was dressed as a little bird, and I thought it was fitting as she flitted about the shop, doing whatever needed doing.

She laughed. "Me too. My husband told me I had better not bring any more candles into the house. But what he doesn't know won't hurt him." She sighed, looking over the display case. "I'm going to go back and see what else your mom wants me to do."

I nodded and rang up another customer. Mom was already working on figuring out who needed to be where when the jewelry shop opened up again. I was looking forward to working there. Looking at jewelry was fun, even if I didn't wear a lot of it. A girl could dream, couldn't she?

We finally got a break from the customers, and I took three empty trays back to the kitchen to be washed. "It's been crazy out there."

Mom nodded. "I don't doubt it. Nina called again. She's worried about the shop, but I told her everything would be fine. I'll stop by and pick up a key from her when I get off."

Grace turned around from where she was washing pans at the sink. "If you need me to go over there and work a shift or two, Ann, I don't mind."

"Would you? I told Nina we would take care of things, so that would be great. I knew I could count on everyone here."

She nodded. "Just say when and I'll be there."

"I'm fine with it, too," Linda said as she got more butter from the refrigerator. "Just let me know."

I set the pans in the sink for Grace to wash, then I got a paper towel and wet it. "I got a little chocolate on myself." I dabbed at it, trying not to make it worse. Dressing as a witch had its advantages. Getting candy on a black costume didn't show as badly as it would on some of my other costumes.

Mom turned to me. "I got a little bit on myself, too."

I laughed. There was chocolate spilled all down the front of her white nurse's uniform. "I didn't even notice. I must be really tired. What did you do?"

She sighed. "I got in a hurry when I was pouring chocolate into a pan to dip bonbons in. I don't know why I didn't put an apron on first."

Grace chuckled. "You work too hard, Ann. With so much on your mind, you just forgot."

Mom nodded. "I suppose so." She looked at me. "Have you heard from Ethan?"

I shook my head, still dabbing at the chocolate. "No. He said he was going to try to clear the jewelry store as soon as he could so Nina wouldn't miss much of the Pumpkin Hollow Day sales. I was hoping he would stop in."

"It must be exciting being married to a detective. I bet he tells you all kinds of stories about his work," Grace said over her shoulder.

I glanced at her. "He tells me a little. But you know how detectives are. They keep some things to themselves."

She nodded. "I should have become a detective. I love a good puzzle. I do all kinds when I get the chance. That's all a murder is, isn't it? Just a really good puzzle."

"That's one way of looking at it," Mom said.

Grace set a pan into the dish drainer. "I hope he can find George's killer. I just can't get over it. Shot right in his own store. I feel so bad for Nina. They both seem really nice."

I dropped the wet paper towel into the trash can. This was the best I could do until I took the costume home and washed it. "Do you know Nina and George?"

"Not really. But I've lived here my whole life, and you know how it is. In a small town, you run into people all the time. Plus I bought my daughter's class ring at the jewelry store."

"That's true. You do run into people all the time," Mom said. "It's why I love living in a small town."

I turned as Ethan walked into the kitchen and sighed. "Hey."

"Hey." I hurried over to him and kissed him. "You look tired."

"I am tired. I just need some fudge to get my energy back. Hi, Ann."

"Ethan, you are going to get a great big piece of fudge. You work so hard," Mom said as she went to cut some for him.

"Ann, you are my favorite mother-in-law," he teased.

Mom laughed, shaking her head. "Oh, Ethan."

I introduced Ethan to Grace. She shut off the water and dried her hands, then shook his. "We were just talking about you. I told Mia it must be exciting being married to a detective. I think you have a cool job."

Ethan smiled. "I tell her all the time that it's exciting being married to me, but she doesn't believe me."

I rolled my eyes. "Don't listen to him."

Mom gave Ethan a large piece of pumpkin spice fudge, and I steered him toward the open back door and out onto the step outside. He took a bite of fudge, nodding. "This is so good."

I nodded. "So? Anything?"

He shrugged. "I've gone over the jewelry store with a fine-tooth comb, and all I found was a vase that had been knocked over, and a pair of gloves. I'm going to ask Nina if she uses them for something."

"What kind of gloves?"

"Surgical gloves. I doubt they belonged to Nina or George."

"Huh," I said. "I've been thinking. Nina said it wasn't a robbery, but maybe the killer got scared off after killing George and before stealing anything. I don't know why they would remove their gloves though."

"Me either. Robbery isn't completely out of the question, although Nina swears nothing is missing." He took another bite of fudge and nodded appreciatively.

I glanced past Ethan and saw Gracie standing near the back door. When she saw me, she moved over to the trash can and began pushing the trash down inside of it as if it was too full. But the can was only half-full because I had dropped a paper towel into it. *Was she eavesdropping?* She walked back to the sink without looking at me.

"Hey."

"What?" I asked.

"I need a kiss before I go back to work. I think it will be late before I get home tonight, so don't wait for me for dinner."

I nodded and kissed him. "I'll probably be working late, too. Maybe I'll grab something quick to eat."

He nodded and kissed me again. "See you later."

I followed him back into the kitchen and Grace didn't look up from the pans and bowls she was washing.

Chapter Five

MY CATS, BOO AND LICORICE, were all too happy to have me home with them that night. I had ordered pizza, and they weren't going to be left out. I gave them each a piece of pepperoni and a bit of the pizza itself with some cheese on it. I ate three slices and eyed a fourth, but decided against it. I didn't need to be up with a stomachache tonight.

I yawned and lit two pumpkin spice candles on the fireplace mantle. Even though it was still summer, I had brought my Halloween decorations out of storage and had worked a bit on decorating the living room this evening. The only bad thing about celebrating Halloween in the summer was that there aren't any fresh pumpkins. Oh well. The assortment that I had in wood, glass, ceramic, and plastic would have to do.

"Meow."

I looked down at Boo. He had slipped off his collar somewhere and needed a replacement. "Yes, Boo?"

He looked up at me expectantly. I shook my head. "No more pizza. I'll give you a cat treat before we go to bed."

He sat and watched as I rummaged through the tote full of decorations. I loved vintage decorations, both authentic and reproductions, and I had tried to collect as many as I could over the years. I picked up an envelope that held authentic vintage cardboard cutouts of cute kids dressed in costumes with their black cats and jack-o'-lanterns and began taping them to the living room window. The cutouts had been taped up for many years, and I didn't want to poke a hole in them to hang them with hooks and suction cups, so tape it was. They were still in remarkably good condition, and I loved them.

I glanced out the window, hoping Ethan would be home soon. If he wasn't, I was going to have to go to bed without him, because I had an early start at the candy store. Christy lived across the street, and her lights were already out. I was a little envious because my feet hurt, and I could barely keep my eyes open.

Licorice rubbed up against my leg, and I reached down to pet her. "It's time for Halloween decorations. I know you can't wait until we can have real jack-o'-lanterns." When Ethan and I got married, and he moved into my cottage along with Licorice, I discovered that she enjoyed a good pumpkin. She spent her days poking her paws through the eyes, nose, and mouth of the carved pumpkins and pulling out what she could for a snack. Thankfully, the pumpkin was good for cats, so we didn't have to worry. But Boo had decided he could do without the pumpkin.

My heart skipped a beat when headlights turned onto the street, and Ethan pulled into the driveway. "Ethan is home."

I went to the door and threw it open, waiting as he wearily got out of his truck and made his way to the front door. He gave me a crooked smile. "Well, hello. Fancy meeting you here."

I chuckled. "It's my favorite hangout." He kissed me, and I squeezed him tight. "Hungry?"

He nodded. "Starving."

"I ordered pizza. Do you want me to warm it up for you?"

He bent down and petted both of the cats. "Nope. I'll eat it cold." He looked around the living room. "You aren't going to wait until October to put up all the decorations?"

I shook my head. "Nope. I'm in the Halloween mood."

He chuckled and nodded, and we headed into the kitchen. "It looks nice. And the candles smell good."

He washed his hands and sat at the table while I put the box of pizza and a plate on the table, and filled a glass with ice and tea and put it in front of him. He was tired, and it showed in his eyes and the fact that he wasn't very talkative tonight.

"I didn't think you would be this late. I could have waited to order the pizza."

He shook his head, taking a piece of pizza from the box. "There's no reason to wait on me. I never know how long I might be when there's a case like this to investigate." He took a bite of pizza and closed his eyes. When he swallowed it, he looked at me. "I am starving."

"I don't doubt it. Long hours like this are hard." I got a glass, and put ice in it and poured some tea for myself. "So, have you found out anything yet?" I went to sit across from him at the table.

He shook his head and took a sip of iced tea. "The chief called in a favor to get George's autopsy done right away, and they pulled a .32 caliber bullet from his chest. They didn't see anything else. No bruises, no cuts. Just the single bullet wound."

"So that means he didn't struggle with his killer. I still can't believe he's dead."

He nodded and helped himself to two more slices of pizza, and I waited until he'd had a couple more bites to say anything else. "I am starving. I might eat the rest of this pizza."

"Go ahead. We'll order another if you want. Did Nina say anything new that might help you with the case?" The cats were winding themselves around his legs, hoping he gave them a bite or two of his pizza.

He shook his head. "Not really. She's sticking to what she told me about finding him."

I looked at him. "What do you mean she's sticking to what she told you? Did you think there was a reason that she might not?"

He shrugged. "Not really. But sometimes people aren't thinking clearly when something like this first happens, and it's not until later that they remember something that might be important. And I have to look at every angle. You know?"

I wasn't sure that I did know. "What are you saying?"

His eyes met mine. "Mia, she was his wife. Plus, she was the last person to see him alive. So many times it's the closest family member that commits the murder, and I have to look carefully at her story."

I probably shouldn't have been surprised, but I was. "As a suspect? Nina?"

He nodded and took a sip of his iced tea. "Between you and me, don't you think it was a little odd that when she got back to the jewelry shop, the door was open, and it didn't set off alarm bells for her? It's true that they have a lot of inexpensive jewelry in there, but they also have some expensive things. Leaving the door unlocked would have been foolish for George to do. I would think that she would have checked on him. Quite frankly, even chew him out for leaving the front of the store unattended."

I inhaled. "I can't see Nina as a suspect. I really can't. She isn't like that."

He nodded. "I know. I really do understand what you're saying. But she was waiting on customers, according to her, while her husband was dead in the back room. When she hadn't heard from him for, say, a half an hour—an hour at the most—shouldn't she have checked on him?"

I felt sick to my stomach. Everything he was saying made sense, but I didn't want to believe any of it. Nina was a good person. I was sure she was exactly who I knew her to be, and that person couldn't kill someone. Especially not her husband.

"But Ethan, do you really think she could have done it? Really? My family has known her for years. I've never seen her do anything that would make me wonder about her character. Never."

He sighed and picked up another piece of pizza from his plate. "I want to believe that. I do. But right now, I have to look at what's in front of me, and she's right in front of me with some suspicious behavior."

I sighed. "What about the surgical gloves? Did they use them at the shop?"

He nodded. "They did. Nina said she wore them when she was handling the more expensive items. She doesn't like to leave fingerprints behind on them. I asked her why she didn't just wipe them down with a jeweler's cloth, and Mia, I am telling you the truth that she looked at me like she was surprised I would ask that."

I stared at him, letting this sink in for a few moments. "So you think that she thought you would believe what she told you without questioning it?"

He nodded and took a bite of his pizza. He closed his eyes while he chewed and swallowed. "Why is this pizza particularly tasty tonight?"

"Because you're so tired. It was really good, though."

He nodded again. "To answer your question, yes. I feel like she was surprised I would ask that, and maybe it was because she wasn't telling the truth. There was a small box of latex gloves in the back room, but it was covered in dust. As if they hadn't been moved or any of the gloves taken out of the box in quite a while."

I sighed. I didn't want to hear this, but it left me wondering. Was I reading her wrong? She seemed to care about her husband. She had said that he was the best thing that ever happened to her. But it was right after she had complained—light-heartedly—that he never wanted to do anything. I closed my eyes and ran a hand across my brow. I was getting a headache.

"Okay, I understand that you have to investigate. I really do. I want you to find George's killer as much as you do. I just hope it isn't Nina."

He nodded. "Me too. I'd rather it be a robbery that fell apart. Maybe they didn't intend to kill anyone, but George spooked them, and they killed him in their panic and then ran from the store without taking anything."

I nodded. "I like that scenario. I hope that's what happened."

I knew Ethan had to look at Nina as a suspect, but that didn't mean that I had to like it. I was going to go on hoping that she was innocent.

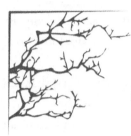

Chapter Six

HEARING ETHAN SAY THAT Nina Black was a suspect in her husband's murder had shaken me. I couldn't imagine how it was even possible that she could have killed her husband, but even I had to admit that things didn't seem quite right with the way she had behaved when she found her shop door unlocked and didn't see her husband out front. George wouldn't have been that careless, regardless of leaving the sign in the window to closed.

I had the early shift at the candy store—4:00 a.m. comes quickly, let me tell you. But a few minutes before nine o'clock, I headed to the jewelry store. Today I was dressed in my favorite gypsy costume—the one with the red calico skirt, and I had a box of candy beneath my arm to share with the girls at the jewelry store. I glanced into the other shop windows as I went. Everyone had decorated their shops with pumpkins, ghosts, bats, and goblins tucked in nearly every nook and cranny. Even though we were several months away from Halloween, I was filled with anticipation. The holidays would be here before I knew it, and I loved all of them.

I pushed open the jewelry store door, and Elizabeth Simpson was behind the counter. She was dressed in a pink bunny costume, and she smiled at me. "Good morning, Mia. Nina told me you would be working here for a few hours today. It was generous of you all to volunteer like that."

I smiled and walked over to her. The sign in the window still said closed, and the shop was empty except for us. "It was the least we could do. Poor Nina is grieving for her husband, and she didn't need the stress of figuring out how she was going to deal with running her shop."

She frowned, and went to the front window and turned the sign over to open. "I agree completely. She needs to spend time with her family, and then there's planning the funeral and the reception afterward." She turned back to me. "I feel so sorry for her. I can't imagine going through something like that. And truthfully, I feel so sad that George was killed. He was a good boss and a good man." Tears came to her eyes as she spoke, and I felt bad for her.

"How long have you worked here?" I knew Nina's other employee, Kelly Jacks because I went to school with her. But Elizabeth was probably in her late forties, and I only knew her well enough to say hello when I stopped in.

She headed back to the front counter. "Two years. It's the best job I've ever had. Nina and George are great to work for. Were." She looked perplexed for a moment. "I don't know how to refer to George anymore. I hate saying that he's gone, or even thinking about it. I just feel lost."

I nodded. "I can totally see how that would be. When you work with someone, you get to know them, and they become friends." Our regular employees—Linda Reid, Lisa Anderson, and Carrie Green were all people that I felt close to, and like they were more than employees. When Lisa left to go to college, it was going to break my heart.

She nodded. "Yes, exactly. But I can't get poor Nina off my mind." She teared up again, shaking her head. "I don't know how she's going to make it through this. I just keep thinking that if it happened to me, I would lose my mind."

"Me too. It's all so horrible and sad."

She sighed. "But Nina is a strong woman, and she will get through this somehow."

I nodded. "I know she will." I held up the box of candy. "Oh, I brought us all a little treat. There's an assortment of candies in here. Help yourself whenever you want."

She smiled, eyeing the box. "Well, isn't that nice of you? Goodness, I love the candy you all make over there." She took the box from me and opened it, but two customers came into the shop before she could eat anything. "Oh. I better wait. Can you put this in the back for me?"

"Sure." I took the box from her while she went to see if the customers needed any help.

I stopped at the entrance to the backroom. George spent most of his time back here, planning their inventory, balancing the books, and whatever else he handled. The flooring back here was linoleum, and I couldn't help thinking about him lying there, bleeding from a gunshot wound. I didn't know who had cleaned up after he was taken away, but I was glad they had done a good job. I sighed and went to the desk, laying the candy box on top.

I glanced around the room. The top of the desk was cleared off, and the boxes of merchandise were neatly closed and on shelves. Everything looked to be in order. I wandered around the room, my shoes making a light clacking sound as I went, and looked things over. There was a safe in the back corner that I knew George had kept expensive items in if there wasn't room out front to display them. Had Nina checked the safe after George was found? A scenario suddenly played out in my mind. Maybe he had been held at gunpoint and was forced to open the safe. Once the robbers had the jewelry and the door had been shut, they shot him. I made a mental note to ask Ethan if he knew whether Nina had checked the safe.

Back out front, more customers came into the shop. I hesitated, not quite sure what to do first. At the candy store, we didn't have to help the customers much outside of cutting fudge or bagging up candy from the display case, and I wondered if it was different here since Elizabeth was helping a customer now.

I left the back room and went behind the front counter and saw that everything was neat and tidy, with bags stacked evenly on the shelves. A few office supplies were lined up on the top shelf beneath the cash register.

"Oh, Mia, could you help those customers, please?" Elizabeth whispered when she came to the front counter to ring up her customer.

"Sure." I headed over to two older women who were looking at charm bracelets. "Hi, how are you ladies today?"

They looked at me and smiled. "Good," one said, and they went back to the charm bracelets, ignoring me.

I hesitated. They seemed to be doing fine on their own, but did Elizabeth think they needed help with something? "Aren't those bracelets cute? I love everything that has a pumpkin or a jack-o'-lantern on it."

The other lady looked at me and nodded. "They are cute." She immediately went back to talking to her friend. I felt like an intruder.

I glanced at Elizabeth, but she was ringing her customer up, and not paying attention to me. Two more customers entered the shop, so I went over to them. "Hello, ladies. How are you doing today?"

"We're doing fine. Lots of fun things to see around this town, and we need souvenirs." She laughed.

"It is a lot of fun visiting this town, isn't it? We have a large variety of souvenirs," I said, motioning toward a wall where Nina kept the less expensive items that people liked to stop in and grab on their way out of town. If you came to Pumpkin Hollow, you needed a souvenir.

"Great, thanks." The two ladies went over to take a look, and I went back to the front counter where Elizabeth was finishing up with a customer.

She turned to me when the customer left. "Oh, Mia, did you see if those customers needed anything?" Elizabeth asked me.

I nodded. "Yes, they just wanted to look around for souvenirs." I leaned against the counter, already tired from the time I had put in at the candy store this morning.

"Well, I like to make sure my customers are being helped. It's good to make sure they know that I'm available. Maybe you can help them?"

I looked at her. It wasn't that I didn't like helping customers, but they all seemed content with doing their shopping on their own. "Sure." This wasn't my store, so I wasn't going to protest. I headed back to the ladies looking at the charm bracelets. "Are you finding everything okay?"

They both turned to look at me. "We're fine," one of them said in a tone that said they really did not want my help. They turned their backs on me. I sighed and went to ask the other two shoppers if they needed help.

WE WERE BUSY FOR THE next hour, but it was nothing compared to what was probably going on at the candy store today, even though it was Monday, and it would be slower everywhere than it was on the weekends. Lots of people were on vacation, and some would be spending it here in Pumpkin Hollow, but weekends were still the busiest time for us.

The shop was finally empty except for Elizabeth and me, and I went to one of the display cases and opened it. There was a cute diamond tennis bracelet that I had my eye on. I took it out of the box and tried it on. "This sure is cute. Very simple, and elegant. I think I need my husband to buy it for me."

Elizabeth glanced at me, closing one of the other display cases. "It's best not to handle the jewelry. It leaves smudges on them."

I put the bracelet back and closed the display case, then I went to the front counter. "That was a nice little rush, wasn't it?"

She nodded absently, her glasses pushed to the end of her nose. She was looking over the cash register tape. "We should have been busier. We haven't taken in that much money." She looked up at me. "Poor Nina will need extra money to bury George, and we've got to make sure she gets it. Can you please try harder to get customers to buy more merchandise? And buy the more expensive items, not the cheap stuff." Her voice cracked, and she was almost sobbing now. I have to say that I was a little surprised by it.

I nodded. "Sure. We don't do a lot of suggestive selling at the candy store because the candy sells itself, but I can try to suggest items that go together." I hated trying to sell things to people. If it didn't seem like something they might want or enjoy, pushing it on them didn't make me feel good. But this wasn't my shop, and I had offered to help out, so I would try harder to do that.

She sighed and gave a quick roll of her eyes. "Yeah, I get that people love candy, and it doesn't take much to sell it. But this is jewelry and souvenirs, and while people do like to buy it, that doesn't mean everyone comes in here all day long like they do the candy store." She slammed the top of the cash register receipt paper closed and went to the back room, leaving me feeling a little dazed. I hurried after her.

"I didn't mean to say that there was anything wrong with suggestive selling. It just isn't something that we do at the candy store." She pressed her lips together, and I knew I had said the wrong thing.

"Thanks, Mia. If you don't want to, you don't have to do it. We'll be fine without your help."

I shook my head. "No, I'm sorry. That didn't come out right. I have no problem with trying to get people to buy more. I know Nina is in a bad spot." I hadn't meant anything by what I said, but now I felt like I needed to explain myself.

She started sobbing now. "All I'm trying to do is help. That's all I'm trying to do. I don't know why you feel like you need to make it harder for me." She brushed past me and went out front as more customers came in. I stood there, stunned, and not really sure what I had done to upset her. But she was dealing with a lot of stress, and maybe it was getting to her. Maybe she felt responsible for helping Nina as much as she could. And she had also lost a boss and a friend, hadn't she? I took a deep breath and went back out front.

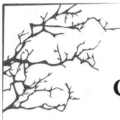

Chapter Seven

THE DAY COULDN'T END early enough for me. What I thought was going to be a fun day at the jewelry store had turned into a mini-nightmare. I'm usually easy to get along with, but I felt like I couldn't do anything right as far as Elizabeth was concerned. So when Kelly showed up for her shift, I was more than ready to go home. But right when I got into my car, Christy texted me and asked if I wanted to meet her at the coffee shop while she was on her break from the candy store.

Coffee. I needed coffee. No way was I turning her down.

"Amanda, please make me the biggest iced vanilla mummy you can make. With a shot of espresso. No, make it two." I sighed. My eyes had begun to close on me while I was driving over, and I needed to make it home in one piece.

One eyebrow rose. "Rough day?"

I nodded. "Rough day. I haven't had any coffee since 4:00 a.m., and I desperately need it."

She chuckled. "For you, anything."

"I love your costume, by the way." Amanda was dressed as Little Bo Peep, and she was as adorable as could be.

"Thanks." She looked past me to the customer behind me in line, but one of her employees called him up to help him. She leaned forward. "I heard about George."

I nodded. "It's so sad for Nina."

She sighed. "I'm going to take a break if you're going to hang out for a minute."

"Sure. Christy is going to meet me here." As I said it, Christy walked through the door. She was dressed as a mummy, but she had begun to unravel. I knew exactly how she felt.

She put her arm around me. "Hey, sis. Buy me a coffee?"

"Sure. What do you want?"

"I'll take a Vampire's kiss. Hot, please." She sighed. "I'm beat. It's been crazy at the candy store, and I've got three hours to go. How was the Jewelry store?"

I sighed and bit back the complaint that sprang up. "Busy. Not like the candy store is busy, but there was a steady stream of customers."

"You're working at the jewelry store?" Amanda asked as she set my drink in front of me.

"Yeah. We volunteered to help Nina out until she could get back on her feet. She has relatives coming into town and the funeral to plan, and we didn't want her to stress about running the shop, too."

"That's so sweet of you." She got a cup and filled it with espresso. "Poor Nina. I can't imagine the heartbreak."

"No, me either," I said. "I don't know what I would do if something like that happened to Ethan." With Ethan being a detective, there were days when the thoughts would come to me that he might not come home. If I didn't deal with those thoughts immediately, I would find myself feeling sad, even though Ethan was just fine.

She nodded. "Devastating." She finished Christy's coffee and then made a small iced coffee for herself, and we went to the corner table to sit and chat for a few minutes.

"Do you think we get an employee discount at the jewelry store?" Christy asked me.

I laughed. "Now you're thinking. But I am not going to ask that question. It's opening Pandora's box." I took a long sip of my drink and sighed. It was perfect.

"What's that supposed to mean?" she asked.

"Yeah, what's that supposed to mean?" Amanda asked.

I shook my head, immediately feeling bad that I had said anything. Elizabeth was going through a stressful situation, and I had no business bad-mouthing her. "Nothing."

Christy blinked. "I know you better than that. What gives?"

"I'm sorry, I shouldn't have said anything." They both looked at me expectantly. "Okay, maybe Elizabeth is a little hard to work with," I whispered.

"Why?" Amanda asked.

I shrugged. "I guess Nina expects her employees to get out on the sales floor and sell. I'm not used to that. It's no big deal, though. This is temporary, and we're doing it to help Nina, and that's what I'm going to do." I felt guilty. I should have kept my mouth shut.

"Great," Christy said. "I'm working there tomorrow."

I shrugged. "Just remember that it's only temporary. It became a mantra for me by the end of the day."

"That bad?" Amanda asked, twirling her straw in her drink.

"Yeah, sort of. But she's under a lot of stress, too. I think Nina's employees are close to both her and George, and losing him is hard on them. I can't imagine it."

Christy nodded, taking a sip of her coffee. "It would be hard. It's heartbreaking that he was murdered. Does Ethan have any leads?"

I shook my head. "Not yet." I wasn't going to bring up the fact that he was looking at Nina as a suspect. I was sure, or at least I hoped, that he would soon realize that she had nothing to do with her husband's murder.

"He'll find the killer," Amanda said.

I nodded. "I know he will." I took a sip of my coffee. "Isabella was so stinkin' cute in the parade Saturday. Did she have fun?"

Amanda grinned. "She loved it. We kept telling the kids to wave and blow kisses, and when people started waving and blowing kisses back, they just ate it up. They're all a bunch of little hams."

"Oh, that is adorable," Christy said. "She's such a cutie."

"Thanks. Oh, and I caught her talking about Ethan the other day. She kept saying, Ethan, where are you? I want to see my Ethan."

"Aw," I said, melting inside. "Tell her I do the same thing when he isn't home. That's so cute."

She nodded. "I'll try to get it on video if she does it again. I wish I had thought to grab my phone."

I chuckled. "Ethan will just fall apart if he sees that. He thinks she's the cutest thing ever."

"That's because she is," Amanda said and laughed. "So what do you think, Mia? Who do you think killed George?"

I sighed. "I wish I knew. It's all so strange. They weren't robbed, but whoever it was slipped into the back room and shot him. Why?"

"I was shocked when I heard about it. He came in the day before he died. In fact, he came in almost every morning to get coffee. I asked him how he was doing, and he seemed—I don't know—distracted, I guess. After I heard he died, I realized that he didn't seem himself that morning."

"Really?" That was odd. "Did he say anything? Was he not feeling well? Or did he mention anyone?"

She thought about it for a moment and then shook her head. "No, I don't think he said anything in particular that was odd. But when he would come in, we always made small talk. Sometimes it was just about the weather, and he left after he got his coffee. But other times he would hang out a few minutes and talk if I didn't have other customers. That morning he almost didn't seem to hear me when I asked how he was and then mentioned the weather." She shrugged. "Maybe it was nothing."

"Maybe it was something," Christy said. "The door to the jewelry shop was unlocked, and the only way it could have been unlocked was by George since Nina said she locked it when she came to get candy and look in the shop windows. He had to have known his killer. Maybe someone was threatening him. Or maybe he did something he shouldn't have, and he was worried about it."

"You have a point," I said. "Maybe he was completely unsuspecting when he opened the door. It could have been a friend that stopped by to say hello, but they weren't really his friend." As I said it, people started flashing through my mind, but I couldn't think of anyone who would want him dead. Maybe Nina had lied about how it had happened, making up a story because she had killed him. I shook the thought away.

"Maybe he did know they were angry at him, but he let them in to try to smooth things over," Christy said.

Amanda nodded. "That's a good idea. I'm betting he did or said something that made someone angry, and he knew it and he was worried. He wasn't himself at all when I was talking to him."

I took a sip of my coffee. "But what would it have been? George was practically a hermit from what Nina says, and he was at the jewelry store working almost every day. So when would he have had the time or the inclination to be around someone he might make angry?"

Christy inhaled. "Maybe it was someone who came into the store. Wait. Doesn't George buy used jewelry from people? Maybe someone brought something in, and he didn't make them an offer they liked."

"You're right. I completely forgot about that," Amanda said. "A few years ago he told me that sometimes people bring junk in to try to sell to him, thinking it was worth a lot of money, and they got angry when he told them it wasn't worth anything."

Now we were getting somewhere. "That's interesting. I forgot about that, too. Nina once told me that people have tried to sell him stolen items, too. But if he felt like something was fishy, he would refuse to buy it from them. He could have made the wrong person angry."

"I think that's it," Amanda said.

"You said he came in almost every morning for coffee. Did he come in for coffee the morning he was killed?"

She shook her head. "I don't remember seeing him."

"So something was bothering him, he didn't do what he normally did the morning that he died, and then he was murdered." I sat back, thinking about this. Maybe he had just made the wrong person angry by telling them their jewelry wasn't worth anything, or he refused to buy something that made him feel uncomfortable. I had to talk to Ethan.

Chapter Eight

"HOW DID THINGS GO?" I asked Christy as she drove us to see Nina. Mom had packed a gift box with two pounds of fudge. Nina would be having guests, and Mom thought it would be nice for her to have some fudge to serve them.

Christy didn't look at me. "Fine."

I eyed her suspiciously. "Fine?" It was her turn to spend the day at the Jewelry store. My sister could be outspoken, and I had the feeling that she and Elizabeth would clash.

She nodded. "Elizabeth and I came to an agreement. We would talk to each other as little as possible, and we would get the job done."

"Oh, no," I said. "What happened?"

She parked in front of Nina's house and turned to me. "I don't like being told what to do. It's not like I don't work in a retail shop every day, and I don't know how to work with customers."

I snorted. "She does like to boss people around, doesn't she?"

She nodded. "Yes, but she isn't going to boss me." She opened the door and got out of the car. I got out on my side.

"Christy, it's only temporary." I was going to work at the jewelry store tomorrow, and I had told myself the same thing every time I wanted to complain about something when I worked there the previous day. Working with someone difficult wasn't any fun, but again, it wasn't going to be forever.

"I know."

She rang the doorbell forcefully, giving away her feelings.

When Nina opened the door, she smiled. "Hi, girls. It's so good to see you. Would you like to come in?" She opened the door wide for us, and we followed her into the living room.

"How are you doing, Nina?" I asked. I held out the box. "Mom sent some fudge."

She smiled warmly and took the box from me. "That's so sweet of her. I love her fudge. And I guess I'm doing as well as I can. I'm still having trouble believing that George is gone. It feels surreal."

I nodded. "I'm sure that feeling will stick around for a while. I'm so sorry."

Her eyes watered, and she grabbed a tissue from the box on the coffee table and dabbed at them. "Have a seat. I can't bear to go through his closet and clean it out. When my sons arrive for the funeral, I'm going to tell them to go through his things and take what they want. I know eventually I'll have to get rid of everything, but I can't think about that now. I'll feel better if they have his things."

"I think that's a good idea," Christy said. "We would want some of our parents' things if one of them died."

She nodded, setting the box of fudge on the table. "Me too. Tell your mother that I appreciate her sending the fudge. My boys grew up here in Pumpkin Hollow, and they always talk about your mother's fudge when they come for a visit."

"We will." I glanced around the room. There were family pictures on the wall, making the room feel warm.

"I sure appreciate you girls helping out at the jewelry store, but I also feel guilty about not being there. George and I got to where we worked most days of the week, and taking time off feels wrong somehow."

I shook my head. "Don't worry about it. You need time to be with your family, and we enjoy working there." Enjoy may have been exaggerating, but it was the thought that we were helping her out that we did enjoy.

She nodded. "I talked to Ethan today, but of course, it's still early in the investigation. I just want to see the killer put away."

"We all do," Christy said. "I hate the idea of a killer being out there somewhere."

"Nina, was there anyone that George was having problems with?" It was something that I had to know. If there was a customer that had issues with how they were treated, then Ethan could look into it.

She shook her head slowly. "You know, the only person I can think of that he had a problem with is Joe Feldman. He owns that small garage at the end of town. Do you girls know him?"

I nodded. "Yes, he's a customer of ours. He comes in every couple of weeks or so. What kind of trouble did George have with him?" Joe wasn't a particularly friendly person. The garage he owned didn't appear to do much business, and the building was dilapidated and the grounds unkempt. I had only taken my car to him one time, and I swore I would never do it again. He kept coming up with more things to fix, and the bill kept growing.

She sighed. "Joe would regularly bring in coins to sell, maybe an occasional piece of jewelry, and he and George got into an argument two months ago. George told him the jewelry he brought in wasn't worth anything, but Joe claimed it had belonged to his grandmother and was an heirloom. Joe didn't want to hear that it wasn't worth anything."

I sighed. Just as I suspected. "What did he say when George told him it was worthless?"

She frowned and sat back on the couch. "Well, George wasn't in a very good mood that morning, and he told him it was trash. Usually, George was better about how he talked to people than that, but as I said, he wasn't in a good mood. And Joe blew up. He accused George of trying to rip him off and said that George didn't have a clue what he was talking about. That made George angry, and before I knew it, they were standing right there in the store, calling each other names. And believe me, they were not quiet about it."

"I bet they weren't," Christy said.

She nodded. "George had bad days occasionally, and I tried to keep him away from the customers when he did. But he's the only one who knows anything about coins and buying jewelry that isn't brand new, so I let him handle those things."

"Why was George having a bad day?" The George I knew was never angry or unkind. At least, not to me he wasn't.

She shrugged and then ran a hand through her hair. "I don't know. I guess he didn't get enough sleep or something. Why do you ask?"

Her tone was clipped when she said it, and I wondered if I hit a nerve.

I shook my head. "I don't know. I didn't mean anything by it. I've always been used to him being happy. But everyone has bad days."

She nodded, relaxing. "George did once in a while. And it was not the first time that Joe came in with something that George knew was junk. There was no way that necklace could have been a family heirloom. It was lightweight and had a funny shine like fake gold does. He had bought it or found it somewhere, and he thought he could fool George. Even I could tell it was junk. It's something that happens sometimes—some people honestly don't know that what they have is junk, but some do."

"Did Joe bring coins and jewelry in often to sell?" Christy asked.

She thought about it for a moment. "At least a couple of times a month. He always got angry when George wouldn't buy something from him. Even if he didn't say so, I could tell by looking at him. Do you think he could have killed George?" She looked at me expectantly.

"I don't really know. I'm not trying to point fingers at anyone. I just wondered if there was someone who might have caused him any problems." I felt guilty now. I never intended to make her suspicious of someone, but I may have just done that.

She sighed and was quiet for a few moments. I wasn't sure if she was going to speak again, and I glanced at Christy.

"I'm sure that Ethan is going to find his killer," Christy said to break the silence. "He knows what a good guy George was, and he won't stop looking until he finds them."

Nina's eyes went to Christy. "George was a good guy. Most of the time. I was lucky to have had him for as long as I did. I feel so lost without him." Her eyes teared up again, and she dabbed at them with the tissue.

"I'm sorry," I said. "I can't imagine how hard this is."

"Me either," Christy said.

She took a deep breath and got to her feet. "I appreciate you girls coming by and bringing the fudge. And I appreciate you taking time out of your schedules to help out at the shop. I've never had friends as good as you two and your mother are. I don't mean to rush you off, but I've really got to get to work figuring out what I want to do for George's funeral. I hate to even think about it."

Christy stood up. "Sometimes we need someone to rely on."

I glanced around the room again as I stood. "If there's anything else you need, don't hesitate to ask."

"Thank you."

She saw us to the door, and when we got in the car, I turned to Christy. "She said George was almost always a good guy. Almost?"

She looked at me. "And it seemed like she took offense to some of your questions. Weird."

I nodded. As much as I didn't want to think about Nina killing her husband, the thought that she may really be the killer kept coming to me. What did she mean by saying he was almost always a good guy? Who said that about their husband after they say how much they loved him and will miss him? Especially after he had been murdered.

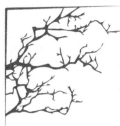

Chapter Nine

"GOOD MORNING, ELIZABETH," I said when I walked through the door of the jewelry store. I made myself smile, and I hoped my voice dripped with enthusiasm because I was not really feeling it. I had scolded myself for my negative attitude three times this morning while getting dressed. There was no reason to act this way, I told myself. Everything was running smoothly this morning, and I finally had my attitude in order before I stepped outside. But then the cats made a run for the door, and I had to catch them before I left, and now I was a few minutes late getting to work, and that aggravated me.

Elizabeth glanced at me but continued helping her customer. I sighed and went to the backroom to put my purse up. I wore a black cat costume today, and I thought it was pretty cute. I had an assortment of costumes in my closet that I regularly switched out with other costumes that were in a storage tote in the tiny shed in the backyard. Our little cottage was small, so closet space was at a premium. It held not only the costumes, but my regular clothes, and now Ethan's clothes as well. I thought my closet was small until Ethan moved in. Then I realized it was teensy.

I headed back onto the sales floor and asked the nearest customer if they needed help, only to be told they were fine. I looked at Elizabeth, who was still helping a customer. She glanced up at me and frowned, then turned back to her customer. I didn't know what I had done to offend her, but whatever it was, it was bad.

Thankfully, we were busy for the next hour and a half, and I didn't need to talk to Elizabeth. That was a good thing. I hated not feeling good about being here and helping Nina out, but I couldn't help it. Elizabeth acted as if she didn't want me here, and Christy had had much the same reception.

Then we were alone in the shop. I smiled. "That was a nice little rush, wasn't it?"

She sighed. "I guess you can consider it little since you have so many customers over at the candy store, but I'd say it was more than little, at least for this store."

I inhaled, telling myself everything was fine. I was doing this to help Nina. "How are you doing today, Elizabeth? I love your costume. Cinderella, right?"

She leaned against the counter. "Belle from Beauty and the Beast. And I'm fine. I'm just tired. Do you know how much responsibility I have trying to keep this place going without Nina and George here to help? When people don't come in on time for their shift, it makes things harder for me."

I hesitated. She in no way looked or behaved like a Disney princess, but I wasn't going to say it. "That's why we volunteered to come work here. We didn't want anyone to have to try to manage it by themselves. You shouldn't feel as if it's all up to you." I ignored the slight about coming in late. It was only three or four minutes, and I wasn't going to leave the cats outside while we were gone.

She made a face. "Look, I appreciate the help. I really do. Without your help, we wouldn't have enough coverage for the store, and we'd have to close, or at least be open fewer hours. Really, I do appreciate it. But let's be honest. The responsibility lies squarely on my shoulders. When Nina comes back, she isn't going to ask you or your mom how things went. She's going to ask me. And then she's going to look at the sales and ask why we didn't sell more."

I opened my mouth to say something and then shut it. Was I really going to get anywhere with her? Probably not. I nodded. "I see your point."

She sighed dramatically. "Finally!" She went to the cash register, and opened the cover to the receipt tape, and started looking over the sales we had done this morning.

I'll admit that I was feeling a little put out by this woman. I had no idea that when we volunteered, we were going to be treated as if we were more a hindrance than a help. I probably would have volunteered anyway, because it was for Nina. But I was having a hard time keeping my mouth shut.

The door opened and I turned toward it, and Joe Feldman walked in. I smiled. Maybe we would get some information from him, if I could get around Elizabeth, that is. "Hello, Joe. How are you this morning?"

He nodded at me and strode right up to the counter as if he had something important to discuss. "Good. Look, I have this ring that my grandfather left me, and I wonder how much you would give me for it." He produced a dirty white handkerchief from his shirt pocket and unwrapped it, showing it to me.

"I'm sorry, we aren't buying any jewelry today," Elizabeth said, looking up from the cash register.

He ignored her. "It's 24 karat gold, and that's a one-carat diamond there. My grandfather said he paid two thousand dollars for it, and that was in 1958. It's got to be worth at least ten thousand or more. Twenty, probably."

I looked at him wide-eyed. Joe was in his fifties, and he wore a dirty blue chambray work shirt and dirty jeans that fit him too loosely. He was balding, and his short brown hair stuck up on his head. "I'm sorry, Joe, but I don't have the authorization to buy any jewelry."

His mouth made a straight line, and he stared at me. Then he shook his head. "Look, I'm not saying I want you to give me twenty thousand dollars. I know you have a business to run, and you need to make a profit, but that is one fine-looking ring, and it will sell faster than any of this other stuff you have in here."

Did he think that I normally worked here? I had waited on him plenty of times at the candy store, and I couldn't imagine him not recognizing me.

Before I could answer him, Elizabeth slammed the cash register shut and elbowed me out of the way. "I said we aren't buying anything today. George has passed away, and he did all the buying." Her voice cracked, and she glared at him. "She doesn't even work here normally. She certainly isn't going to be making any decisions about anything."

He blinked. "Well, where's the woman that's usually here? She'll buy it from me."

I doubted it. The band of the ring was made of chunky gold, and the diamond was smaller than one carat, even if he thought otherwise. I couldn't tell if it was real gold or a real diamond, but it didn't look like a valuable family heirloom. Not that I was an expert. I knew very little about jewelry, but it didn't look valuable at all.

Beth sighed, closing her eyes. When she opened them, she smiled. "Mr. Feldman, I'm sure you can appreciate how Mrs. Black is at home grieving over her dead husband. She isn't going to be buying anything anytime soon."

He slammed his hand onto the glass countertop, causing me to jump. "I don't care about anyone dying. I want to sell my ring."

If Elizabeth was afraid of him, she didn't let it show. "Sorry. There's nothing I can do for you."

Two customers walked into the shop, and she abandoned me to help them. I swallowed, looking up at Joe. He was a large man, over six feet tall and at least three hundred pounds, and he was angry. *Thanks a lot, Elizabeth.*

He narrowed his eyes at me. "I need you to buy this ring."

I shook my head. "I'm sorry, Joe, but just like Elizabeth said, I don't even work here normally. I'm just helping out after George died. I can't buy anything from you."

He stood up straight, grabbing the ring and wrapping it in the handkerchief. "This place is as useless as can be. If George were here, he would buy it from me, and for a good price, too.

They need to just shut it down if they don't care nothin' about their customers."

Suddenly, Elizabeth was back at the front counter. "You'll have to leave, Mr. Feldman."

He snorted. "Make me."

Her mouth dropped open. Finally, she had an appropriate reaction to the situation. "Don't you talk to me that way. I'll call the police if you don't leave."

I slipped away to the back room while they argued about whether he was going to leave or not, and I called Ethan. "Can you come to the jewelry store?"

"Sure. What's going on?"

"We have a customer that is angry and won't leave."

"I'm two blocks away. I'll be right there."

I hung up and took a deep breath. I could hear Joe arguing that he wanted money for the ring and Elizabeth arguing just as loudly that he was not going to get any. Is this what George put up with from him? And why did a mechanic have so much jewelry and coins to sell that he came in once or twice a month?

A moment later, I heard the front door open, and I went to the doorway and looked out as the two customers that were in the shop hurried out, and Ethan walked in. Joe glanced over his shoulder to see who had entered, then turned back. He frowned.

"Joe, how are things going?" Ethan asked and came to the front counter to stand beside him.

He shoved the ring into his pocket and nodded. "Great. I was just trying to sell a piece of jewelry, but I've got to get going now."

"I told him we couldn't buy it, and he became belligerent," Elizabeth said.

Ethan looked at him. "Is that right, Joe?"

He shook his head. "Nope. Just a little misunderstanding. I've got to get back to work. I'll be seeing you around."

Ethan watched him walk out the door.

"Why aren't you arresting him?" Elizabeth demanded.

He turned to her. "Did he commit a crime?"

She gasped. "He tried to intimidate me and make me buy something I didn't want. He came in here all the time and tried that with George."

I went over to Ethan. "He was getting pretty obnoxious."

"If he didn't commit a crime, I can't arrest him. But if he comes back and behaves that way again, I'll see what I can do."

Elizabeth rolled her eyes. "That isn't going to do us any good. He should be in jail. He's so disgusting. He probably killed George. If you were doing your job, you would know that."

That was not going to fly with Ethan. I had told him what Nina had said about Joe, and if he felt he needed to talk to him about the murder, he would.

"I'm sorry you don't think I'm doing my job. If you can do it better, then I guess you should." He kept his eyes on her, waiting for a response.

Elizabeth turned pink, shaking her head slowly. "I'm sorry. I shouldn't have said that. I'm just flustered by what he did."

Ethan nodded. "Give me a call if he comes back."

He turned to me, his eyes wide. "Let's go out front." When we were outside, he chuckled. "Sounds like you're not having a great day."

"You're telling me. Joe was kind of scary though. He never acts that way when he comes to the candy store."

"Because he knows you don't buy jewelry. I'll stop by the garage and talk to him. See if he knows anything about George's murder."

"Good. It was weird that he didn't even react when Elizabeth told him George had died."

"Maybe he already knew. I've got to get back to work." He leaned over and kissed me. "I was just going to Amanda's to get some coffee. Want me to pick one up for you and bring it back?"

I nodded. "Yes, please. Something with ice and a couple of shots of espresso?" I was consuming a lot of caffeine the past few days, and I did not care. It was getting me through the day.

"I'll be right back."

I watched as he headed in the direction he had come from. I was surprised by how Joe had behaved. If he was acting that way with George, then I did wonder if he had killed him because George wouldn't buy something he wanted to sell. I shivered and went back inside.

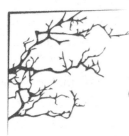

Chapter Ten

"HOW ARE THINGS GOING at the jewelry store?" Mom asked as she spread pumpkin spice fudge evenly into the pan. Next, she would make little swirls on top of it and then let it cool.

I yawned. "Sorry. It's going as well as can be expected, I guess." I took four pounds of butter from the refrigerator and put them on the counter. We needed more vanilla fudge. It was a customer favorite, no matter the time of year.

"You sound tired," Linda said. She was dressed as a witch and was packing candy orders to be shipped out.

"I am exhausted. Getting up early is not my thing." I went back to the refrigerator and took out the cream.

"Are you sure things are okay over there?" Mom asked, then stopped to straighten her clown wig.

I nodded. "It's fine. We'll get through this. They just do things differently over there, and it takes a little adjustment period, is all." Or maybe a long adjustment period. Thankfully, I wouldn't be there long enough for the adjustment to happen.

Mom nodded. "I'm glad things are going okay. Nina called last night and asked about everyone, and I told her you girls were doing great. She's worried about the shop, but her sons flew in with their families, and I told her to enjoy visiting with them and the grandkids. There's no need to hurry back."

I nodded. "That's the most important thing. For her to spend time with her family."

"I still can't get over it. George Black is dead," Linda said. "He and Nina have always been so nice, and it just isn't right."

"It certainly isn't," Mom said. She came over to the counter where I was assembling the vanilla fudge ingredients. "I'll take over making the fudge if you'll run to the bakery and get us a dozen donuts and some coffee. I think we could all use some coffee."

"Sure. Maybe going for a walk will help me to wake up. What kind of coffee do you both want?"

"Oh, I would love a vanilla latte," Linda said. "And any kind of donut. You know me. I'm not picky about my pastries." She laughed.

I grinned. "Me either. I love my donuts far too much to get picky about them."

Mom got a clean wooden spoon from the drawer to spread the fudge with when she was done. "Vanilla latte sounds good. Just get a mixed dozen of donuts. I'm sure the other girls will want one when they come in. There's cash in my wallet."

"I'll be right back." I got some money from Mom's purse and then headed to the bakery. It was still early, just after seven o'clock, and the air was cool outside. It felt good to go for a walk with the town still quiet and serene before the tourists arrived.

When I got to the bakery, there was a small line of customers, but it didn't take long for Angela Karis to get them served and on their way.

She smiled when I got to the front of the line. "Good morning, Mia. How are you today?"

I nodded. "I'm tired and in need of some coffee. And so are Mom and Linda. Can I get three vanilla lattes? With a shot of espresso in one of them, please?"

"Coming right up."

I peered into the display case. The donuts looked so good. "Can I also get a dozen donuts? An assortment of whatever you want is fine." I leaned on the front counter and inhaled the scent of the fresh baked goods. My stomach growled in anticipation.

She got to work on the lattes first. "So, I heard about George Black. Sure is a shame."

I nodded. "It really is. I never would have thought that someone would murder him, of all people."

She nodded, the wig she wore for her unicorn costume bobbing with the motion. "I know what you mean. Who would have thought it?"

I stepped back and straightened my costume—I was Dorothy from the Wizard of Oz—then I looked into the display case again. She had iced sugar cookies that she had carefully drawn Halloween scenes onto with colored icing. "These cookies must take forever to make. They're really cute."

She chuckled. "They do, but I love making them. I make one big batch each morning, and when they're gone, they're gone. Did I tell you that Vincent got me a couple of employees to help out?"

"No, you didn't. I don't know how you were doing so much work practically by yourself before."

She nodded. "I told him I couldn't do it anymore. Jessica Bannon is in the back, making more donuts as we speak. I'm in heaven." She laughed again.

"I bet you are."

Angela had taken over at the bakery when Vince Moretti's wife had died, and she had been doing almost all the work by herself. Vince showed up and helped out, but I had the feeling he probably didn't do a lot, and the part-time employees they used to have had all left for one reason or another. She had been working almost solo for months.

She put the lids on the lattes and brought them to the counter. "So tell me, Mia, has Ethan found George's killer?"

I hesitated. There was a time that I didn't like Angela much, but I had changed my mind about her. Sort of. She was still the town's biggest gossip, and I had to be careful with what I said, or it would be all over town as soon as I walked out the door.

I shook my head. "Not yet, but you know how things go. Sometimes it takes a while for a killer to be caught."

She nodded. "Yes, I know it does take time." She picked up a bakery box from behind the counter and unfolded it. "Has he spoken to George and Nina's employees? Maybe they know something that was going on that George was worried about."

I nodded. "Yes, he's talked to them. I'm not sure what the result was." Actually, I did. They were not aware of anyone that might have had something against him and would want to kill him. But after the experience I had working at the jewelry store yesterday, I had my eye on Joe Feldman.

She slid open the door to the display case and picked up a sheet of waxed paper to pick up the donuts with. "Just an assortment?"

I nodded. "Yes, you know how we love your donuts. I don't think there are any that we don't like." Angela had decorated the donuts with Halloween themes. The boo-berry was my current favorite, followed closely by the chocolate werewolf, which was just a chocolate donut with ears and whiskers piped on. It was darn cute, though.

She began filling the box with donuts, and she glanced at me. "I heard that it was a robbery. But not just any kind of robbery. It was organized by one of their employees." She looked at me meaningfully.

I shook my head. "Nothing was stolen, so it couldn't be a robbery." Did she have some actual facts, or was she just talking? Angela liked to be the center of attention.

She shrugged and put two boo-berry donuts in the box. "I heard it was Elizabeth Simpson who organized a robbery, only it wasn't supposed to end in murder." She eyed me.

My stomach did a flip-flop. "Where did you hear that?"

She shrugged again. "You know how it is around here. People talk all the time. I forget who told me that."

I fiddled with the necklace that I wore. She was lying. She knew exactly who had told her, but she wasn't going to tell me. That's how gossips were. They liked to spread things around, but you could never pin them down to the facts of where they got the information.

"If it was an employee—Elizabeth—she could have stolen things from the store when George wasn't there. She and Kelly close the shop by themselves, and they have a key."

She hesitated, a werewolf donut suspended above the box. "I suppose that's true. But maybe they wanted to get back at George for something. Maybe the murder was planned."

I shook my head. "I don't think so. Elizabeth and Kelly enjoy working for the Blacks. I've only heard good things from them about their employers."

She nodded and picked up a Frankenstein bar and carefully placed it into the box. "I bet they are, and were, good people to work for. I liked George, and I like Nina. But if you want to hear something juicy, I can tell you what was really going on down there."

I wanted to sigh and roll my eyes. I hated playing games like this, and it reminded me why I hadn't liked Angela at first. I shrugged. "What?"

She grinned. "I heard Elizabeth had the hots for George."

The idea of this made me sick. But I knew it wasn't true. George was faithful to his wife. He was not the sort of man that would cheat on her. I felt confident about this. "I don't think that's true. George was not like that."

She shrugged and put two more donuts into the box. "All I know is what I heard. But you didn't hear it from me if you know what I mean."

That was the problem. Gossips liked to spread the trash around, but they only wanted credit for it when it was no longer gossip. Then they bragged that they had told you it was true. I wasn't falling for it. George wasn't that kind of man.

"I think someone is mistaken about that. If you can't say who told you, that's because it isn't true."

She shrugged and finished filling the box, still grinning because I had fallen for her game. "Here we are. A baker's dozen." She went to the cash register and rang me up.

"Thanks, Angela. I'll see you later."

She nodded. "I know you will. Have a good day."

I hurried out with my lattes in a cardboard carrier and the box of donuts in my hands. Angela was lying, wasn't she? She had to be. When someone was afraid of something being attached to their name, it was because they were lying.

Chapter Eleven

GEORGE BLACK'S FUNERAL was well attended, just as I thought it would be. It seemed like most of the business owners had made it. Nina had asked us to close the jewelry store and put a sign on the front letting people know that was where we were today. It was a good idea. This meant that both Elizabeth and Kelly could attend, as well as my family. My dad had taken the day off from work, and he came with Mom to support Nina and her family.

Mom and Dad sat in the pew in front of us at the First Baptist Church, while Christy and her boyfriend, Devon, sat next to me and Ethan. Amanda and her husband Brian sat on the other side of Ethan.

The front pew was filled with George's family, which included seven grandchildren. I hadn't realized that he and Nina had that many grandchildren. As I looked over the crowd, I saw a lot of familiar faces. When you own a business in a small town, everyone knows you, and it didn't surprise me that so many people had shown up, even though George was an introvert who rarely ventured outside of his home or business.

On the far side of the sanctuary Elizabeth sat rigidly in the pew. She appeared to be alone as she sat facing forward and didn't talk to anyone. Kelly was on the opposite side of the sanctuary. If it were me and any of our employees, we would have sat together. I wondered if Kelly had chosen not to sit with her because she was so bossy at work.

Ethan took my hand and squeezed it. He smiled as he leaned over. "You don't have to figure out who killed him. That's my job."

I shook my head, smiling. "I'm just looking over the crowd while we wait for the service to begin."

"Sure."

I shook my head. There was little chance I was going to stop thinking about who might be the killer at this point in my life. I had been doing it for too long.

My dad turned to us. "A lot of people turned out today."

I nodded. "I'm glad. For his family's sake."

"Yeah, I'm sure it will make them feel a little better," Christy said.

He nodded and turned forward again. Sighing, I laid my head on Ethan's arm. I hated funerals. Especially when it was for someone who wasn't ready to go yet. Unfortunately, that wasn't uncommon, but I didn't have to be happy about it.

The pastor took the podium, and I sat up.

WHEN THE SERVICE ENDED, we made our way to the front to hug Nina, weaving back and forth between people as some headed out of the sanctuary. There was a meal afterward in the fellowship hall, but I wasn't sure if we were going to go or not.

When we finally made it to the front, I looked away from the open casket. I wanted to remember George as he had been, not as he was after the mortician had fixed him up.

"Mia, Ethan, thank you for coming," Nina said and hugged me. "I'm glad you both could make it."

"We wouldn't miss it for anything. How are you doing?" I held her at arm's length. There were dark circles beneath her eyes, but she looked like she was holding up.

She nodded. "As well as I can. Having my kids here helps a lot."

"I'm sure it does. I'll see you later, and we'll catch up." She hugged Ethan, and he whispered something to her, and she nodded. The line behind me was backing up, and we had to move on so others could talk to her. Christy and Devon, and Amanda and Brian were behind us, and they took a moment to speak to Nina, while Mom and Dad had gone ahead of us.

We patiently waited for the mass of people to move toward the doors, inching our way along the aisle. Polly Givens and her husband Carl were standing at the end of a pew, and I waved to her. When we got to her, I paused for a moment and hugged her.

"Fancy meeting you here," she said.

I nodded. "It's a good turnout, but it's so sad that we all showed up for this and not something happier." Polly and Carl owned the gift shop and had been friends with our family for years.

She nodded. "I still can't believe it. Ethan, how are you doing?"

"I'm good, Polly."

She nodded. "I hope you find the killer soon."

"Me, too."

Polly squeezed my hand as we moved on. When we finally made it out of the crowded sanctuary and outside, I spotted someone I knew standing near a tree. "I want to say hello to Kelly." Kelly worked for Nina, but I had only had the misfortune of working with Elizabeth. I wanted to see how she was doing and if she might mention anything that might help figure out who killed George.

"Hi, Kelly," I said and hugged her. "I saw you inside, but it's so packed that I couldn't get to you."

She nodded, smiling. "It was a good turnout. George would have appreciated it. Hey, Ethan." Christy and Devon had stopped to talk to someone, and we were alone with her.

"Kelly, I know you must miss George. I'm sorry for your loss."

She nodded appreciatively. "He was a good boss. I'm going to miss him. Nina is a good boss, too, and I feel so bad for her."

"I was hoping I was going to get to work with you at the jewelry store, but it hasn't happened yet," I said.

She nodded. "Elizabeth is making me work the late shift." She rolled her eyes, and at that moment, Elizabeth walked by. She glanced at us, but she didn't stop to talk. "I hope she didn't hear me," Kelly whispered when she was out of earshot.

Ethan shook his head. "I don't think she did. She didn't act like it."

Kelly leaned against the tree. "Just because she didn't act like it doesn't mean she didn't. She's a wily one. You have to keep your eye on her."

"Really?" I asked.

She chuckled. "I'm exaggerating. Elizabeth is okay, but not my favorite person to work with."

I nodded. "Too bossy?"

"Exactly. But I guess you already know that. How long are you going to be filling in at the jewelry store? I'd love to get to work with you. It would be fun."

I shrugged. "I'm not sure if my mother has talked to Nina about how long she's going to be gone. I guess there's no rush. Pumpkin Hollow Days will be over in a week, and things will slow down at the candy store."

She nodded, and when a car backfired, we all turned toward the parking lot. I spotted Grace Andrews pulling out of the parking lot in an old pickup.

"Someone needs to have some work done on that truck," Ethan said.

"That's Grace. I didn't notice her before the service began." Actually, I thought she was supposed to be working at the candy store. I could have been wrong about it, though.

"It was hard to see who all was here, there were so many people," Kelly pointed out.

"I'm going to go say hello to Adam Phillips over there," Ethan said when he spotted an old high school friend of his. "Kelly, it was good seeing you."

"You too, Ethan."

I looked at her after he left. "Kelly, can I ask you something? I don't want to keep you, but there's something I wondered about."

She nodded. "Sure. I'm waiting for my husband to pick me up, and he said he would be a few minutes."

I stepped closer. "Have you ever thought that Elizabeth might have had an interest in George?" What Angela had told me bothered me. I didn't think it could be true, but what if I was wrong? I had told Ethan, and he thought Angela was just gossiping, and if anyone knew for sure, it had to be Kelly.

Her brow furrowed. "An interest? Like, a romantic interest?"

I nodded, feeling funny for even asking. "It's probably just gossip."

She laughed. "I don't know if she had an interest in him or not, but believe me, he would never have had an interest in her. George wasn't the romantic type. I'm pretty sure it would have required too much energy to look outside his marriage for something like that. Not to speak badly of him, I mean. He was a good guy. It's just that I couldn't imagine him even thinking about someone else."

I nodded. "I thought the same thing."

"Why? Who told you that?"

Now I felt bad. I was just as guilty of gossip as Angela was. "I'd rather not say. I don't think it's going around. At least, I hope not." Knowing Angela, it probably was, but there wasn't anything I could do about that.

She shook her head. "I just can't see it."

I glanced over my shoulder, but no one was close enough to overhear our conversation. "Beth is the controlling type, isn't she? I feel like I can't do anything right."

She laughed again. "Welcome to my world. I don't know what it is about that woman, but she likes to be the boss. She's worked there a few months longer than I have, and she likes to remind me of it. I guess she's just that kind of person."

"Why do you stay? I've only worked with her a couple of times, and it left me wanting to give someone my resignation."

She nodded. "I know. There are days I've felt the same way, but I don't think she even realizes what she's doing. And like I said, Nina and George are good people to work for, so I put up with Elizabeth, and the occasional surly customer."

That reminded me about Joe. "Did Joe Feldman come in often and give George a hard time when he didn't want to buy jewelry from him?"

She rolled her eyes. "That one thinks he's slick. Most of the time he thinks he's got something worth thousands of dollars, but it's junk. George would tell him he wasn't going to buy it, and Joe would throw a fit, and then leave. We would see him a couple of weeks later, and he would do it again. Occasionally he has something worth a little money, and George would buy it from him, but whatever it was, it was never very valuable. Probably less than a hundred dollars."

"Interesting."

A car pulled into the parking lot and drove alongside us, and the driver waved at Kelly. "I gotta go. It's been good talking to you, Mia. I hope we get to work together soon."

"Me too. See you later."

Christy and Devon came up to me. "I'm starving," Christy said. "Are we going to go to the reception?"

"I don't know. Let's check with Ethan. If he doesn't want to do that, we can go to lunch."

"That sounds good," Devon said.

I was glad I had talked to Kelly. It confirmed what I knew about Angela and her rumors and also made me a little less scared that Joe Feldman was going to lose his temper one day and shoot us.

Chapter Twelve

"GOOD MORNING, EVERYONE," Grace sang as she hurried through the kitchen and into the break room to put her purse up. When she reappeared, she was tying an apron on over her 1950s-style outfit, complete with a cute pink poodle skirt and black and white saddle shoes. It was a darling costume, and I was a little envious. I needed a poodle skirt.

"Good morning, Grace," Mom said. She was watching the large stand mixer as it whipped the pumpkin spice fudge to perfection. "How was it working at the jewelry store?"

"Fantastic. I got to talk to a bunch of customers who were souvenir hunting, and I worked with Kelly. Kelly was a lot of fun." Grace had worked the day after the funeral, and now I was jealous that she had gotten to work with Kelly.

"Lucky you," Christy said, setting a pot into the dish drainer. I laughed. "Now, Christy."

She turned to look at me. "What? I didn't say anything."

Mom chuckled. We had filled her in on the troubles we were having working with Elizabeth, but we had tried not to spread our complaints to the rest of the employees here. That was the last thing Nina needed to hear, should it ever get out. I didn't resent helping her one bit. I just didn't like working with Elizabeth.

"You girls are doing a good thing," Mom said. "I'm proud of all of you."

"I enjoyed it," Grace said. "If anyone wants me to work for them over there, I don't mind."

"Me!" Christy called over her shoulder as she rinsed a mixing bowl.

I shook my head and turned to Grace. "You left the funeral so quickly the other day that we didn't get a chance to say hello."

Her brow furrowed. "Funeral?"

I hesitated. "Yeah. George's funeral. It was nice of you to attend. I'm sure it made Nina feel loved for so many people to show up."

"It was a comfort to her, I'm sure," Mom said, turning the mixer off.

Grace shook her head. "I didn't go to George's funeral. I took a personal day. My son had a doctor's appointment at 11:30 that morning. Did you think I went?"

I looked at her. I had seen her in that old truck, hadn't I? And then I realized that I had never seen her driving that truck before. She drove a car. I shook my head. "I could have sworn I saw you in an old truck. It was red."

She shrugged and smiled. "I don't own a red truck. My husband has a black one, but I almost never drive it. Maybe it was someone who kind of looks like me?"

Was it someone else? I swore it wasn't. But why would she lie about it? "I guess I made a mistake." I looked up, and Christy was watching me.

Grace chuckled. "Mia, you might need glasses. I had to be at the doctor's office at the time the funeral was being held. Ann, what do you want me to do? I'm raring to go after two days off, and I can do anything you need."

Mom smiled. "Why don't you take over for Christy at the sink? She's been washing dishes and pans all morning. She probably needs a break."

"You betcha," Grace said.

Mom looked at me. "You girls can take a break if you'd like."

Before I could answer her, the phone on the wall rang, and I reached over and answered it. "Pumpkin Hollow Candy Store. How may I help you?"

"Is this Mia?" a woman asked.

"Yes."

"Mia, this is Nina. Is your mother there?"

"Of course, hold on, Nina." I handed the phone to my mother.

"Hello, Nina," Mom said. Then there was silence for a few moments. "I had no idea." More silence, then "let me take this call in the office." She set the phone on the counter. "Mia, when I pick up the phone in the office, will you hang this one up?"

"Sure." She hurried into the office and closed the door.

Christy and Grace watched her, then Christy turned to me. "What's that about?"

I shrugged. "I have no idea."

ICED COFFEE WAS EXACTLY what I needed. Christy and I walked to Amanda's coffee shop, and we bought iced werewolves for ourselves and the other employees who were working this morning. We were disappointed that Amanda wasn't at work, so we decided to walk slowly back to the candy store, looking into the shop windows as we went.

"I love Halloween," Christy said as we looked into the display window that Polly had set up. She had a cute collection of Jack-o'-lanterns and pumpkins.

"You had better, or you're living in the wrong town."

She chuckled, and we moved on to the flower shop. Frankie Malone had beautiful displays of fall flowers she had brought in from a supplier that grew them especially for her. If you didn't know what the calendar said, you would think it was October as you gazed at her displays.

"Is that Mom?"

I looked down the sidewalk at the woman coming toward us. "Yes."

She was hurrying as she walked, and we walked faster to meet her.

"Mom, what's going on?" I asked, hoping there hadn't been an accident. She looked worried, and the pace she was setting made my heart beat a little faster.

She stopped in front of us and breathed in, trying to catch her breath. She held up one finger.

"We brought you an iced coffee," Christy said, handing it to her. "What's wrong? Did something bad happen?"

She shook her head and took a sip of the iced coffee. "I hope not. I don't know."

"What is it?" I asked.

She took another deep breath, then steered us over to one of the benches that lined the street. Christy and I sat together and turned toward her as she sat, turning toward us. "Nina is upset. She wanted to know why I sent Grace to work in her store. I told her she volunteered to do it."

I shook my head. "And? She wanted us to help her out."

She took a deep breath and released it. "She didn't realize that Grace worked for us. Three years ago, Grace worked for her at the jewelry store, and she fired her."

I felt a little nauseous. "Why did she fire her?"

Mom was quiet for a moment. "For stealing."

"What?" Christy exclaimed. "Are you sure? Grace? Our Grace?"

"But she's always so sweet and helpful. She's never been in a bad mood, and she shows up on time. She volunteered to go down there and work to help Nina out." Even as I was saying it, I knew how silly it was. None of those things had anything to do with whether she was a thief or not. I couldn't wrap my head around what she was saying.

"That has to be a mistake," Christy said. She was struggling as much as I was with this bit of information.

"What did she steal?" I asked.

"She said at first it was just small things. Souvenirs, costume jewelry, that kind of thing. She thought she had to be wrong about it and that someone had to have sold the missing items. But then she realized that couldn't be right. The cash register records the item numbers in its computer and when she searched for the items, some of them hadn't been sold. She still wanted to believe Grace wasn't stealing, so she didn't do anything about it. But then a Rolex went missing. Since she didn't have any proof Grace had taken it, she let her go for not showing up on time. I guess that was an issue for her back then. But the real reason was that she thought she was stealing from her."

"And no one else could have taken it?" Christy asked.

She shook her head. "No. Grace was working the front, and George was in the back that day. Nina had worked a few hours in the morning and left, so there was no one else. You know the expensive watches are kept locked in a display case, so a customer couldn't have done it, either."

My heart sank. "She volunteered so she could steal something else, didn't she?"

"I don't know." She took a sip of her iced coffee. "Nina was so upset, and I felt so bad about it. I wouldn't have allowed her to go if I had known. I never would have hired her."

"Why didn't Elizabeth or Kelly tell us about her when she showed up to work there?" Christy asked.

"Because if it was three years ago, she was fired before either Kelly or Elizabeth were hired. I bet they didn't know about her, and Nina and George probably didn't talk about what had happened in front of them," I said. We sat quietly for a few minutes, trying to process this. I liked Grace. We all did. Could she really have done this?

"I feel, I don't know—cheated. I know that doesn't make sense. But she left the jewelry store off her job application so we wouldn't check with Nina, and she's been so nice, and we trusted her," Christy said, breaking the silence.

Mom put her hand on hers and squeezed it. "Maybe she's changed. Maybe getting fired from the jewelry store made her think about what she was doing."

"We haven't been missing anything," I said. "And the cash register has balanced every night since we hired her. I think if she stole from Nina, she would steal from us. Don't you think so?"

Mom nodded. "That's why I think she's changed. Or at least, I hope she has."

"What are you going to do about it?" Christy asked.

She shook her head. "I don't know. She's been a good employee, and I hate to hold her past against her. But I don't want to give her the opportunity to steal any cash from the register, either."

"I agree." During an event like Pumpkin Hollow Days, we took in a lot of cash, especially on the weekends. If she stole the day's money, it would hurt in more ways than one. "Maybe we should get back to the store."

Christy nodded. "I'll say."

We got up and headed back. Linda was at the store working the front, and I knew she would keep an eye on things. I wasn't sure I wanted Grace to stay. And she had to be lying about being at George's funeral, but why? I hadn't made a mistake about seeing her. Was she angry she was fired? Did she want to see for herself that he was dead? It didn't add up.

Chapter Thirteen

"WHAT DO YOU THINK?"

I was leaning back against the kitchen counter at the candy store, and I had just spilled everything that had happened with Grace to Ethan. I was in turn, angry and then hurt. She had lied to me when she said she wasn't at George's funeral, hadn't she? But why? And worst of all, I was worried that she might have stolen something from Nina's store when she went to help over there. The expensive items were kept locked up, so I doubted Elizabeth or Kelly would have allowed her to have the keys since she was only there filling in, and she wasn't an actual employee. But even some of the costume jewelry could be priced moderately high, and if she grabbed a handful, it would hurt Nina.

He sighed, pressing his lips together as he thought about it. "Are you certain that you saw her at the funeral? I know you said you did when we were out front, but when I looked, all I saw was the back of an old pickup."

I crossed my arms in front of me. "I swear it was her. I know she said she took her son to the doctor, but I believe it was her."

"Has she ever driven that pickup to work?" he asked.

I shook my head. "No. She drives a car, and her husband drives a black pickup. But maybe her car wasn't running, and she borrowed it from someone." There had to be a reason she was driving it instead of her car. And then an idea came to me. "Maybe she borrowed it so no one would recognize her in it." I may have been grasping at straws, but it seemed possible.

"Maybe."

"I just can't believe that she lied to us," Christy said. Her arms were folded across her chest, and she stood next to Mom. All the employees had left for the day, and I had called Ethan to come here so we could tell him what had happened.

"I think you can fire someone for lying on their application," Ethan said, looking at Mom. "If that's what you want to do."

Mom shook her head. "I don't know what I want to do. She's been such a good employee. She's only temporary, so I don't even have to have a reason to let her go. But you know me. I can't stand to be unfair to anyone. Letting a good employee go doesn't sit right with me."

"But Mom," Christy protested. "She lied. And if she lied, there's no telling what else she might do. What if she decides to take money from the cash register?"

"I know," Mom said with a sigh. "But firing someone isn't something I enjoy doing."

I picked up a cup that was used earlier during the day and set it in the sink. "No one expects you to enjoy firing someone. I just hope everything is all right at the jewelry store. I can't stand that she lied to us, but this is a small town. Did she think Nina would never come into the candy store? And when she did and saw her working here that she might say something to you? She should have been honest on her application."

Mom's brow furrowed. "So you think I should fire her, too?"

I hesitated. Was that what I wanted? "I don't even know what I want. But she didn't bat an eye when she lied about not being at the funeral. And Ethan, the day after George was murdered—when we went out onto the back step to talk—I swear she was eavesdropping on us. When I turned around, she was standing right there by the trash can, and when she saw me looking at her, she pretended she had thrown something away and was pressing down the trash because it was too full, but it was only half full. I had just thrown a paper towel in there when we walked outside, so I know there was no reason to be doing that."

He nodded. "Then it might be best to let her go. And I think I'm going to talk to her about George's murder."

"You think she murdered him?" Christy asked.

He shrugged. "I don't know, but it's odd behavior. I don't know what her motive would be unless she's still angry that she got fired. Did Nina say who actually fired her from the jewelry store, Ann?"

Mom thought about it for a moment. "I'm pretty sure she said that George did, but I can't swear to that."

He nodded. "All right. It's probably best that she isn't working here when I go talk to her. She might become angry and take it out on all of you."

Christy snorted. "I don't want her around after you talk to her. She may shoot us all."

He chuckled. "Don't get paranoid, Christy. We don't know that she's the killer."

"I hope she isn't. I would hate to see her go to prison," Mom said. "She really is nice."

"I don't want to see her go to prison, either, but if she killed George, she has to," I said. I yawned, glancing at the clock. It was almost ten o'clock, and I was ready to go home and go to bed. "Why don't we go home, and we can figure out how we want to handle this tomorrow?"

Mom nodded. "That's a good idea. I'm tired."

We had already taken care of the closing work, so we headed out to the front door together. Ethan took my hand and squeezed it. "Want to stop and get something to eat?"

"Absolutely."

WHEN WE DROVE PAST the jewelry store, the lights were still on, and I could see Nina inside. I pointed her out to Ethan, and he immediately pulled over in front of the store. The street was quiet this late at night, and when Ethan knocked on the glass door, Nina jumped.

"It's Ethan and Mia!" he called, hoping she could hear him.

Nina nodded and hurried to the door, unlocking it and pushing it open. "What are you two doing out here this late?"

"It was a late day for both of us, and we're headed to get something for dinner," Ethan said. "How are you doing, Nina? What are you doing at your shop this late?"

She sighed, frowning. "I suppose Mia told you about Grace?"

"I'm so sorry about that, Nina. We never would have allowed her to work here if we had known." I still felt bad about that happening, even though we didn't know.

She shook her head. "It's not your fault. I know it isn't. I'm just angry at that little sneak. I hope I wasn't too rough on your mother. I really appreciate all she's done for me, and I probably sounded ungrateful."

"Mom knows you would never be ungrateful. We're all sorry that Grace did that. If we had any idea you had fired her for stealing, we would never have hired her."

"Are you missing anything?" Ethan asked her.

Her lips pressed together. "Maybe. There was a diamond bracelet missing from the display case. It doesn't show as being sold, but someone might have rung it up under the wrong number."

"What did it look like?" I asked, hoping I could remember if I had sold it.

"It was a tennis bracelet set in silver. The diamonds were small, so it wasn't expensive; just two hundred dollars. But now I'm worried she took it. I'll ask Kelly and Elizabeth if they sold it. It was the only one I had, so they should remember."

I had admired the bracelet in the display case. "I think I know which one you're talking about. I know I didn't sell it, but I'll ask Christy if she did."

"I'm going to talk to Grace," Ethan said. "If no one sold the bracelet, let me know, and I'll see what she says about it."

She nodded. "I hate to make trouble, and if I had any doubts about Grace before, this is removing them."

"I'm just so sorry this happened," I told her. If Grace stole that bracelet, I was going to go from being hurt that she had lied to very angry.

"Thank you. I think I'm going to go home. My kids are still in town, and I would like to spend as much time with them as I can."

"I'll walk you to your car," Ethan said.

She went inside and got her purse, and then stepped outside and locked the door. Her car was parked at the corner, and Ethan walked her to it. They talked for a minute, and then Ethan came back to the truck.

"I am going to talk to Grace, and it may not be pretty."

I nodded. "I can't believe someone would have the nerve to do what she's done. First, she lies on her application by not putting down the jewelry store, then she volunteers to help out there just so she can steal more jewelry? After the store owner has just lost her husband? And maybe she's the one who killed him?" The more I thought about it, the angrier I got.

"Slow down there, Babe. We don't know if she killed George or if she stole the bracelet. First things first. We'll figure out how to handle letting her go so your mom doesn't have to get too stressed out about it, then I'll talk to her."

"She's just going to lie about it," I grumbled. "And if Christy and I are there when you talk to her, we'll have something to say."

He chuckled as he backed out of the parking space. "You and Christy are not going to be there when I talk to her. I'll handle it."

I sighed. "Fine. But I am starving right now. Let's get something to eat before I faint."

"You got it."

Chapter Fourteen

THE FOLLOWING MORNING, I was at the jewelry store ten minutes before opening. I was dressed as a clown—a costume that I rarely wore, mostly because clowns creeped me out a little. But it had been marked down seventy-five percent after the Halloween season had ended three years ago, and I love a bargain. Plus, it came with a pink wig, and who doesn't like pink?

I knocked on the glass door to let Elizabeth know I was there. When she didn't answer, I cupped my hands together against the glass and peered inside. I spotted her hanging up pumpkin-themed souvenirs on a wall. I knocked again and waited, shifting the jumpsuit-type costume so the pink and orange patch pockets were aligned correctly. One of the reasons it was on sale, I discovered later, was that the seams were off just a bit. It was enough to keep me on guard against twisting, as well as to keep me straightening it.

When she still didn't come to the door, I knocked harder. Maybe she had some earbuds in that I couldn't see. The sun was on my back, and I was beginning to sweat a little in this nylon costume. Sometimes a bargain isn't that much of a bargain. I knocked harder and jiggled the door in its frame. Finally, she looked up at me and scowled. I waved. She could scowl all she wanted; I was here to help Nina.

She unlocked the door and jerked it open. "What? There's no reason to be so impatient!"

"I'm not impatient. I just couldn't understand why you couldn't walk twenty feet to unlock the door for me." Yeah, I know. I should have kept my mouth shut, but it was hot out here.

She huffed and stomped back to the display. "Do you think you can clean up the backroom? It needs to be swept and mopped, and the bathroom needs cleaning."

"Sure. I'll do whatever needs done."

She glared at me, and I knew she wasn't finished. "I hope your mother isn't sending your friend over here again. Nina told me about her. George would be appalled that you would do that to her."

I stopped in my tracks. "My mother isn't a mind reader. We had no idea that Nina wouldn't want her to work here, and I'm sure Nina doesn't want this talked about to just anyone." I said the last part because I wanted her to keep quiet about it. It didn't concern her what had happened. It was between my mother and Nina. And if she wanted to start in on my mother, I was going to handle that.

She snorted. "Poor George would roll over in his grave if he knew what was happening at his store."

I wanted to reply to this, but the door opened, and the first of the customers entered the store.

Elizabeth rushed over to her. "Good morning, and welcome. Is there something I can help you with?"

I rolled my eyes and headed to the back. Normally I tried to be pleasant to my co-workers, but Elizabeth was proving to be a difficult person to work with. There was a drawer that we put purses in, and I put mine in there.

I was growing tired of the way Elizabeth treated Christy and me. We only wanted to help, but it seemed like we couldn't do anything right. I took a deep breath and went to the corner of the room where a mop and broom leaned. If I stayed back here, I could avoid her, so cleaning the bathroom was a small price to pay.

I got to work sweeping the floor. Pumpkin Hollow Days were almost over. I hadn't taken a day off since it began, and I was looking forward to finally being able to sleep in late and not think about working. Anywhere. As I swept, I glanced at the open door that led to the sales floor. I heard the front door open and close a few times, and I wondered if Elizabeth might need some help with the customers. Then I decided against it. If she needed me, she could come find me.

Mom had texted me this morning that she was going to handle things with Grace, but she wanted some time to get up the courage to do it. I felt bad for her. Mom was such a gentle soul that firing someone would break her heart. She had only done it two other times in her life, and she hated it. My grandmother had been the opposite of my mother in personality. She was strong-willed and spoke her mind. It would have been nice to have her around now because she wouldn't have had a problem firing Grace. But she passed away when I was fifteen, and I still missed her every day. Her influence was all over the candy store and couldn't be missed. It was a comfort to us.

I had the back room and bathroom floors swept, and I was getting ready to mop when I thought I should at least let Elizabeth know that the floors would be wet in case she needed back here for something.

I headed out front. Elizabeth was waiting on a short line of customers, and I hurried over to help her. At the candy store, we worked as a team to move the line quickly and get people on their way. I picked up a bag from beneath the counter and began putting the customer's purchases inside of it.

"What are you doing?" Elizabeth asked and stopped ringing up the souvenirs her customer was purchasing. There was a large assortment of Pumpkin Hollow merchandise on the counter in front of her.

I glanced at Elizabeth but didn't stop. "Helping you with the line so the customers don't have to wait so long."

"I can handle the line. I thought you were working on cleaning in the back?"

I turned and looked at her. Was she really doing this in front of the customers? "Customers appreciate being waited on quickly."

"I'm fine."

It took everything in me to keep from saying something I knew I would regret, but I decided to be the bigger person and set the bag down. "The backroom and bathroom floors will be wet for a while." I turned and headed back. If she needed the bathroom, she was out of luck.

I pulled my phone from my pocket to fire off a text to Ethan about not being appreciated and then changed my mind. He was busy, and I wasn't doing this for Elizabeth anyway. I headed back for the mop and bucket and got started by pouring pine cleaner and water in the bucket, complaining silently as I went. I needed a day off to get my attitude right.

The bathroom was small and only took a few minutes. From the looks of everything, Nina kept things clean, so there wasn't anything difficult about what I was doing. But I was ready to be back at the candy store permanently.

Next, I worked on the backroom floor, leaving a walking path in case something was needed back here. When I got to the area where the safe was, I noticed it had a layer of dust along the top, so I leaned the mop against the wall and got the duster. That was when I remembered that I had forgotten to ask Ethan whether Nina had checked the safe to make sure the killer hadn't taken anything from it. The safe was old, black, and about four feet tall by three feet wide. There was no way anyone could have walked off with it. I supposed if several people wanted to move it and they had some time, they could. Otherwise, that thing wasn't going anywhere.

I dusted the entire safe, then put the duster up. When I went back for the mop, I stopped in front of the safe. Certainly by this time, Nina would have checked the safe. Especially since she was worried that Grace may have stolen from her. I went back to mopping, but I kept looking at the safe. It looked vintage. Was it just for looks, or were Nina and George keeping merchandise in there?

I ran a finger along the top of it. It was cool looking with its gold print, and I wondered how old it was. Had it been here when they opened the jewelry store? A remnant of another business that had been here long ago? I put my hand on the top of it. I couldn't resist. I turned the dial, and it clicked softly as it turned.

"What are you doing?"

I jumped and spun around, suddenly feeling like I had gotten caught with my hand in the cookie jar. I shook my head. "Nothing. Mopping."

She narrowed her eyes at me. "Why would you need to be near the safe if you're just mopping?"

I smiled nervously. I suddenly felt guilty, but I didn't have a reason to. "Because there's a floor beneath the safe, and it needs to be cleaned around it. There was also dust on the safe."

She pressed her lips together, boring a hole into me with her eyes. "I think you need to go."

"What? What are you talking about?" My heart was pounding in my chest, but there was no reason for it to do that. I breathed in, trying to steady it.

"I can handle the store by myself. Thanks for all your help, but you can tell your mother that we won't be needing any more help."

"That isn't your decision," I said, feeling shaky. "That decision was made between Nina and my mother."

She shook her head. "Nina left me in charge. George always relied on me to take care of things, too, and it's ridiculous to think that any of you candy people could understand what to do around here. Not to mention the fact that you sent a thief over here. Do you really think Nina needs that kind of stress right now?"

Candy people? I stared at her. She was being ridiculous.

"Get out."

That was it. I was done. I leaned the mop against the wall, grabbed my purse, and headed out the door without saying another word to her.

Chapter Fifteen

I WAS ANGRY. THERE was no way to deny it. Ordinarily, I wasn't an angry person, but I was making an exception today. I was also starving, and I decided that a trip to the bakery might help me calm down. Eating my feelings was something I tried to avoid, but not today. Besides that, a little walk would help me feel better.

There were three other customers in line ahead of me at the bakery, all ordering something Halloween-themed. I texted Christy while I waited and told her we needed to talk when I got to the candy store and asked if she wanted a donut and some coffee. The answer to that was yes, of course. Not surprising. If there was one thing we could all agree on at the candy store, it was that we loved our donuts and coffee.

"Hi Mia, how are you this morning?" Angela asked when I got to the front of the line.

"I'm doing great," I lied. I was not going to spread around the fact that I was kicked out of the jewelry store and told my help wasn't wanted. I was going to be hurt over that for a while.

"What can I get for you? And I love your costume. It's so colorful, and any costume that comes with a wig or a hat is always fun. I love them."

I smiled, exhaling as quietly as I could so she wouldn't suspect anything. "Thanks. I like yours, too." She was dressed as an orange cat, and it looked good on her.

"How is Ethan doing with the murder investigation?"

"Oh, you know how it is. He's working on it. Why don't you give me five iced vanilla lattes and a dozen donuts? Anything is fine for the donuts. They're all delicious, and they won't go to waste."

She grinned. "Coming right up. I guess your mother has a full crew working this morning. Five?"

I nodded. "Yes, everyone wants fudge. Especially pumpkin spice." We had only planned on four employees to work this morning, but since I was displaced from the job where it was planned that I would work, there were five of us.

"Oh, your mother's pumpkin spice fudge is my favorite. I love it. I've got to get some before Pumpkin Hollow Days ends, or I am going to be sad." She got to work on the iced coffees. The bakery didn't have a variety of coffee drinks, but they made up for it with donuts. I loved the donuts here.

"Thanks, Angela."

She nodded and put a lid on one of the cups. "I heard that someone has been stealing from the jewelry store." She clucked, keeping her eyes on me for a reaction.

I wanted to scream. Who was spreading this around? I shrugged and smiled instead. "I hadn't heard that."

She nodded. "Seems a shame. First someone kills George, and now they're stealing from the jewelry store? People are so awful these days. They don't care about anyone but themselves."

"That's the truth." I felt sick that someone was talking about the missing bracelet from Nina's shop. I was sure it couldn't have come from anyone at the candy store, so it had to be Nina or one of her employees. At least, I hoped it didn't come from anyone at the candy store.

She shook her head. "I also heard that awful Joe Feldman said he couldn't stand George. Said he was ripping him off when he tried to get him to buy his coins and jewelry."

"Oh? Did he say that?" I tried to sound uninterested, but I was interested. What else did Joe have to say?

She nodded, grinning again. "Vince took his car to Joe's garage yesterday morning. I told him not to take it there. The Pumpkin Hollow Garage is a lot more honest, but you know Vince. He does his own thing. Anyway, Joe told him all about it. Said he hated him, and that George ripped him off, but you know that isn't true. Vince was wondering if he might have killed George. I told him that it wouldn't surprise me. That Joe is just a little off if you know what I mean." She put a lid on another coffee, still looking at me for my reaction.

"Some people don't know that it's wrong to speak ill of the dead."

She chuckled. "That Joe probably doesn't know a lot of things. Like I said, he's off. I don't know how he keeps that garage open. Most people don't like him, and the place is a mess and falling apart. I feel dirty even going in there. If I were Ethan,

I'd keep my eye on him. According to Vince, he really hated George. Said he got what he deserved."

He got what he deserved?

I nodded. "I'm sure Ethan has been talking to a lot of people." I was going to keep it at that. Who he talked to about the murder was his business. And mine when I wanted to ask around.

She finished with the iced coffees and got a bakery box out for the donuts. "What about you? Who do you think might have killed George? It's all anyone is talking about, you know."

I shrugged and shook my head. "To be honest, I've been working so many hours since Pumpkin Hollow Days began that I haven't had much time for anything else." That was the absolute truth. I was tired.

She nodded and began filling the box with donuts. "Sure is a shame. George's killer out on the loose still. I'm glad the tourists don't seem to have heard about the murder. I'd hate for them to be scared off."

I smiled again. If she thought I was going to slip and tell her something that she could spread around, she was out of her mind. "Yes."

She set the box of donuts on the counter and began ringing up them along with the coffee. "I guess things will settle down after Pumpkin Hollow Days are over. Maybe then Ethan will find the killer."

I nodded and paid her. "Thanks, Angela. I had better get going." For a moment, I had to think about how to carry everything. The drink carrier only held four coffees. I managed to hold the handle and the extra drink in one hand and the box in the other, balancing them all together in front of me while Angela held the door for me.

"See you later."

"See you."

I hurried down the sidewalk. I had managed to escape without letting anything slip. Joe Feldman thought that George got what he deserved? Ethan needed to know about that.

The anger I felt about being asked to leave the jewelry store had dissipated and in its place was embarrassment that I had been caught touching the safe. Not just touching it, but turning the dial. How was I going to explain that? I didn't even know why I had done it.

Thankfully, there were only four customers at the candy store when I got there. I held up the coffees for Linda to see as she waited on an older woman who was buying what looked like five pounds of saltwater taffy. Linda smiled and nodded. She was dressed as a witch again today.

When I walked into the kitchen, I held up the coffees again and opened my mouth to announce that we had treats, but Christy turned and looked at me wide-eyed. Loud voices came from the office, and the door was closed.

"What's going on?" I whispered and hurried to the counter to set everything down.

"Grace," she whispered, coming to my side. "Mom decided to let her go today."

"Today? I thought she was going to wait?"

She shrugged, and the office door was thrown open, slamming against the wall.

"I can't believe you did this to me, Ann!" Grace cried. But it wasn't tears, it was anger. I might have known a little bit about how she felt. I had been asked to leave today, too. Only, her dismissal was permanent.

"Grace—," Mom said from behind her.

Grace stopped when she saw Christy and me. "I bet you two are behind this. And after I did so much for you all! I even cleaned the bathroom every shift. I have never been treated so disrespectfully in all my life."

I shook my head and could feel the wig move with the motion, feeling like it was coming loose from the hairpins I had used to hold it in place. "Grace, we didn't do anything."

She was seething now. I could almost see the steam coming from her ears. "Someday, the two of you will pay for this. Do you hear me? None of you know anything about running a business or dealing with employees. You all stink!"

Mom's face was pale, and I knew this was one of the worst things she had ever had to deal with here. She took a deep breath. "Grace, we discussed why I had to let you go. I don't like doing this. I think you're a hard worker, but I can't trust you. You didn't tell the truth."

She turned around and said some things that were completely unnecessary, and then she stormed out onto the sales floor. Christy and I followed after her to make sure that she left. More customers had entered the shop by this time, and Grace stopped in the middle of the store. "This is the worst place in the entire world to work! They treat their employees like dirt! And the kitchen where that candy is made is filthy. I wouldn't eat a bite of it." She turned and gave me a look of triumph. As if that had sealed our fate in the candy business. She headed for the door and slammed into it, pushing it open, and was gone.

The customers watched her go, then turned back to Christy and me.

I shook my head. "I'm sorry you all had to witness that. It was completely uncalled for. And the kitchen isn't filthy. If any of you would like to come back and take a look, you'll see that we keep the kitchen immaculately clean here at the candy store." I waited while they processed this. Simply telling them it was clean was not going to convince them, but offering to let them take a look would show them that what Grace had said was a lie.

"You're all welcome to come back and look," Christy said, coming to my side.

"I've been eating candy here for years, and it's always been the best. If this place was filthy, I would have gotten sick at some point. I don't believe a word she said," a woman dressed as a bat said and put two chocolate pumpkins on the counter and then looked into the display case. Her words were like a balm as relief spread to the other customers. Linda looked at us wide-eyed, and I shrugged. We went back into the kitchen.

"Well, that went well," Mom said as she dabbed at her eyes with a tissue.

"Oh, Mom," I said, and we went to hug her. "Don't take it personally."

"Yeah, she made the decision to lie," Christy pointed out.

I was shocked that Grace could behave this way. And it made me wonder. Had she behaved this way when she was fired from the jewelry store? And had she vowed to pay George back like she just did to Christy and me?

Chapter Sixteen

AS SOON AS GRACE LEFT, I texted Ethan and asked him to come to the candy store. Mom was upset, and Christy and I tried to tell her that none of this was her fault, but she was having a hard time accepting it. Grace could spread it all over town that our kitchen was dirty, but this was Pumpkin Hollow. We were well known here, not just as a candy store, but on a personal level. No one was going to believe that our kitchen was filthy. Those that did could do without delicious, handmade candy.

Ethan looked at me after we had explained what had happened and what Grace had said. "Well, she doesn't handle getting fired very well."

"She threatened us," Christy pointed out. "She probably did the same to George when he fired her."

I nodded. "She has to be the killer." We had shut the kitchen door so none of the customers could hear our discussion. I was angry, and I was tired. If Grace was George's killer, then I wanted Ethan to arrest her so we could put this behind us.

He nodded and came over to the counter, his eye on the box of donuts. "I don't suppose I can have one of these? I know it's a cliché for a cop to be eating donuts, but I've been so busy that I haven't eaten anything today."

"Not only can you have a donut, but you can have an iced vanilla latte. Grace isn't here to drink it." I grinned.

He chuckled and opened the box of donuts. "This is my lucky day."

"I guess I should have waited to fire her," Mom finally said. "Maybe it would have gone better if it was at the end of the night when there are fewer customers in the shop."

Ethan picked out a ghost donut and looked at her. "I would have come and hung out. It's not like I'm not here a lot anyway."

"She wouldn't have dared to act like that with you here," Christy said.

Mom sighed. "I should have thought about that, but I just kept thinking that I needed to get it over and done with. Otherwise, I would worry myself sick over it. Now I can worry myself sick over being threatened and her telling people our kitchen is filthy."

He shook his head. "No, you don't have to worry about that. I'm going to talk to her. And if she comes around or harasses you all in any way, I'm going to handle it."

I leaned against him as he took a sip of his iced coffee. "It's been a long day."

"It certainly has," Christy agreed. She came over and looked through the box of donuts. "I'm glad you brought these. I need one. Or three." She picked out a werewolf donut and an iced coffee and stood on the other side of Ethan.

"I think she killed George," I said, taking a sip of my iced coffee. "The way she acted was so unlike her. Or unlike who I thought she was. But she lied about who she was, so I guess it shouldn't surprise us."

Ethan nodded. "I haven't talked to her yet, but I'm going to. It sounds like she has some real issues, and if those issues made her kill George, then I am going to find out about it, and she is going to a place where they don't allow you to throw fits like that." He winked at me.

I snorted, shaking my head. "I bet she gets over having fits real quick in jail."

There was a knock on the kitchen door, and we all turned toward it. Mom was the closest, so she opened it. "Nina. How are you doing?"

"I'm not sure, Ann. Am I interrupting anything? Or can I come in?"

"Of course you can come in." Mom held the door open for Nina, then closed it behind her.

Nina looked tired. There were dark circles beneath her eyes, and it looked like she had been crying. She looked at Ethan. "I hate to interrupt."

"You're not interrupting anything," Ethan said. "Is this something you wanted to talk to the ladies about? I probably need to get back to work anyway."

She shook her head and looked at me. "You're welcome to stay, Ethan. Mia, I just got a call from Elizabeth. She said you were trying to break into the safe in the backroom."

The floor felt like it dropped out from beneath me. I hadn't had a chance to tell anyone what had happened at the jewelry store. I shook my head. "Nina, I would never do anything like that. Elizabeth sent me back there to clean, and I noticed the safe was dusty, so I dusted it. I thought it was an interesting old safe. It looks like an antique. So yes, I did turn the dial, but that was it. I had no business touching it, and I apologize."

She sighed, crossing her arms in front of herself. "I appreciate everyone helping out at the shop. I do. But Elizabeth said that you tried on the bracelet that I'm missing. I still can't find it, and neither Elizabeth nor Kelly sold it."

I stared at her. Did she think I stole it? Me? Ethan took a deep breath beside me. "Nina, are you saying that you think I stole the bracelet? Because I would never do that. And besides, I could have bought it if I wanted it. It's true that I tried it on, but that's all I did."

She closed her eyes for a moment, then opened them. "I don't know what to believe anymore."

Ethan was quiet. I knew what he was doing. He was taking all of this in before he said anything. That's the way he was. I wished I was more like him. "I can't believe you think that I stole from you. I have never stolen anything in my life. I don't know what Elizabeth's problem is, but for some reason, she doesn't like me, so I guess I shouldn't be surprised that she said something like that. But you've known me for years, Nina. How could you think that?" Tears sprang to my eyes. The events of today were just a bit too much for me.

"Mia would never do something like that," Christy said in my defense.

"Nina, do you really think Mia could do something like that?" Ethan asked. "Steal a bracelet? I'd have bought it for her if she wanted it, or she would have bought it herself."

Nina looked at us, and then she started crying. "I just don't know what to do. I wish George were here. He would know how to handle all of this."

Mom went to her and hugged her. "We know you're doing your best."

I felt bad for Nina. I really did. But I was hurt that she could even entertain the idea that I had stolen something from her. I put my hand on the back of my neck. I was getting a headache.

"Did Elizabeth really say that Mia stole the bracelet and that she was trying to break into the safe?" Ethan asked.

Nina looked up at him, and Mom handed her a tissue. She nodded. "She said she didn't want to believe it, but since no one had sold it, it had to be her. She said she noticed it missing the day Mia tried it on, but she thought Mia had sold it and didn't think much of it. Until I told her about Grace and how upset I was about her coming to work here while I wasn't there. That was when I realized it was missing. Elizabeth didn't say anything about it at first, but when she caught Mia trying to open the safe, she realized that she had to have stolen it."

"I was not trying to open the safe," I protested. "I just thought it was interesting, and I turned the dial. She was hateful to me when she told me to get out, and she never stopped to find out what was really happening." I knew I was innocent of stealing the bracelet and of trying to open the safe, but it didn't take away my embarrassment at having been caught turning the dial on the safe. It was none of my business, and I should have left it alone.

"I don't know what to believe anymore. I'm going to go back to work." She turned to Ann. "I appreciate all you've done, Ann. Really, I do. But I can take it from here."

Mom nodded. "All right, Nina. If there's anything you need, let me know, and I'll try to help."

Nina nodded and left without acknowledging the rest of us.

"Can you believe that?" Christy hissed when the door closed behind her. "How can she think you did something like that?"

I shook my head and cried. "I don't know. This is such a mess. Mom, if you don't mind, do you think I can go home for the day?"

She nodded. "Of course. This has been a trying day."

"Mom, why don't you go home, too?" Christy suggested. "It's a weekday, and it won't be that busy. Carrie comes in at 1:00, and Linda and I will be fine."

She hesitated, then nodded. "That's not a bad idea. I could use some downtime."

I was devastated that Nina could think I might have stolen from her, but I was worn out from everything that had happened today that all I wanted was to go home and take a nap.

Chapter Seventeen

I WENT HOME AND TOOK that nap. Surprisingly, I slept for three hours. After my nap, I lay on the couch with the cats and mindlessly changed channels on the tv, pausing occasionally when something looked interesting. I hadn't even thought about making anything for dinner when Ethan came home early, surprising me and the cats.

"Hey," he said and leaned over and kissed me. "How are you?"

"I'm fine. How did you manage to escape so early?"

He sat down on the edge of the couch. "I figured that I needed to spend some time with my wife, who hasn't been treated very well lately. Life. It gets rough sometimes."

I chuckled. "I'll be all right. I can't be angry with Nina. At least, not for very long. She's been through so much, and I can't expect her to be thinking clearly. Because she isn't thinking clearly. She knows me better than that."

He nodded. "I know. I have some bad news. Between you and me."

I groaned. "Oh, come on, I don't need any more bad news."

"I know. We can skip it." He stood up and went to the kitchen doorway. "I don't smell any deliciousness coming from this kitchen. Why don't we go out for dinner? It's been forever since we did that."

I groaned again. "That means I have to brush my hair. And you can't tell me you have bad news and then walk away. What is it?" I didn't want to hear any more bad news, but it would drive me crazy now that I knew some existed.

He turned around. "Nina took out a life insurance policy on George."

I sat up. "And?"

"She did it three months ago. For a million dollars."

I gasped. "A million? Seriously? Who takes out a million-dollar life insurance policy on someone who isn't rich or famous?" I realized what I had just said. "No, I didn't mean it that way. You know what I mean. Usually, those kinds of policies are taken out on people who are actors or actresses, or someone who has something special about them that makes them worth more." I was just digging that hole deeper. I didn't mean anything against George, it just seemed like a lot of money.

He laughed. "I think it's a lot of money for most people to buy. And then to have him murdered so soon afterward makes me think something is up."

"You still think that Nina murdered him?"

"I'm not completely convinced, but this is another nail in the proverbial coffin."

"Who told you about it? Are you just thinking it's her because of what she did today? Because if you are, you don't need to. She's been under a lot of stress lately with George being murdered, and I know she doesn't mean it." Even after hearing Nina say that she thought I may have stolen from her, I couldn't believe that she would do something like kill her husband.

He shook his head and came back to sit down. "She mentioned the policy yesterday. And no, I am not suspicious of her because she sort of accused my adorable wife of theft. I just think it's a lot of life insurance to put on someone, and then that someone ends up murdered. Their kids are grown, so it's not like she needed the money to take care of them. The jewelry store has insurance on it, I'm sure. So why so much money?"

"Did you ask her?"

He nodded. "I did. She said that George insisted that if he should die, he wanted her to live in luxury for the rest of her life."

"Really," I said, thinking. "I'm assuming the reason no one heard a gunshot is that there was a suppressor on it. Did they own guns?"

He shook his head. "No."

"And in California, there's a waiting period to buy a gun."

"Yup. Plus a thorough background check. And before you ask, I checked up on it, and she did not buy a gun recently. Not legally, anyway."

I shook my head and got to my feet. This was something to think about, but it could wait. "I'm starving. Where are we going to go?" I headed to the bathroom to brush my hair and check my makeup. It's amazing how one little nap can make you look like a clown without having to wear a wig.

WE WENT TO A RESTAURANT that served American food just outside of town. The Vampires' Lair boasted freshly baked bread and mouthwatering desserts, so how could we miss?

"What are you getting?" I asked, looking over the menu. I wasn't sure what I was ordering, but I was starving, so I wanted it to be something hearty. We'd been served our drinks and promised that when the waitress showed up, she would bring a basket of that warm, freshly baked bread that was making the whole place smell so good.

"I don't know. They have a Hawaiian burger that looks good."

"Their burgers are always good," I said. "I think I want the Halloween hijinks pot roast. It has potatoes, carrots, and pearl onions swimming in gravy." My stomach growled, and I may have been just a little excited when the waitress showed up with the bread. She was dressed as a vampire, as all the waitstaff were. In the off-season, they wore t-shirts with the restaurant logo on them, but since this was Pumpkin Hollow Days, they wore costumes. The cape was shortened so there wouldn't be any accidents as they moved about the tables.

"Hi Mia, hi Ethan, fancy meeting you two here," Sarah Bogle said, setting a basket of warm bread on the table. We had gone to high school with Sarah.

"Hey, Sarah," Ethan said. "We know this place has some of the best food in town, so we had to stop by."

She chuckled. "It is pretty tasty. I haven't seen you two in forever. What's going on with you guys?"

"You know how it is. We're trying to survive Pumpkin Hollow Days, just like you are. It's packed in here." I glanced around. If we had waited to leave the house any later, we would have had to wait for a table.

She nodded. "It's been like this since before Pumpkin Hollow Days began. My poor feet have been screaming at me. And I need to get into the candy store and get some pumpkin spice fudge before it's gone. What can I get for you tonight?"

"I'm going to have the Halloween hijinks pot roast. I'm starving."

She jotted it down on her order pad. "Halloween hijinks pot roast is really good. You won't be at all hungry after that." She turned to Ethan.

"I think I'm going with the totem pole Hawaiian burger with a side of fries."

"You got it." She wrote it down and glanced over her shoulder, then turned back. "Do you mind me being nosy?"

"No, go ahead," Ethan said. I grabbed the breadbasket and buttered a piece of bread. I was too hungry to wait any longer.

She leaned in. "George Black's murder—I was wondering how it was going." She glanced over her shoulder again, but everyone was either busy serving or talking to their tablemates.

"Oh, it's going. Why?" he asked.

She hesitated. "Well, I know that he and Nina had problems in their marriage. My sister worked for them for about three months last fall, and she said they argued all the time."

Ethan nodded. "I guess that happens sometimes."

"I know. It probably sounds like nothing. But they have that weird woman working for them. Elizabeth Simpson. My sister, Elise, said she would lean on George in the backroom sometimes. She walked in on them several times, and they would jump and move away from each other. Maybe I shouldn't have brought it up, but I was thinking that maybe Nina caught them, and she killed him."

I sat up. I'd heard that Elizabeth had a thing for George, but I didn't believe it. Was I wrong? Had Nina caught them together? It would be sad if they really were getting too close to one another right there in the jewelry store where Nina might see it for herself.

Ethan was quiet for a moment. "What else was Elizabeth doing? Besides leaning on him?"

"She was controlling. That's why my sister quit. She couldn't take it. When Nina was there, she was better, but when Nina left for the day or left to run errands, Elizabeth would immediately start up, telling her what to do, and criticizing everything she did. She said she couldn't take it anymore and quit."

Ethan nodded. "I've heard some of these things, but no one has provided proof that Elizabeth and George were really fooling around. I will definitely keep it in mind."

She nodded. "Maybe it's nothing. It's just that Elise was so convinced they were having an affair. She said Nina has a terrible temper and that she just knew she would get back at them if she found out. That's another reason she quit. She didn't want to be there when it happened." She shrugged. "I just thought I should say something. I'll go turn your order in to the kitchen."

"I appreciate the information," he said.

I passed him a plate with a buttered piece of bread. The yeasty goodness was wonderfully warm and made me think of the holidays. "What do you think?"

"I think Nina has as good a reason to kill her husband as anyone does. It's hard for me to believe George had an affair, though."

"I agree. I think we're still missing something."

I would never believe that George could have had an affair. It just wasn't who he was. And as for him and Nina having marital problems? Maybe. But sometimes couples went through stuff like that. It didn't mean someone was going to end up dead.

Chapter Eighteen

HAVING DINNER OUT WITH Ethan had been just what I needed. We spent most of the evening talking about us, and our future, and not the murder. It was the breath of fresh air that I needed. And knowing that I wouldn't have to go back to the jewelry store was more of a mood lifter than I thought it could be. It was then that I realized just how much I couldn't stand working with Elizabeth. I was disappointed that I never got to work with Kelly, but that couldn't be helped. I was back at the candy store making fudge, and that was all that mattered.

I carefully spread the hot fudge onto a pan so it could cool and then be cut. I inhaled. "I still can't get over how good this fudge smells. I think I'll feel this way no matter how many years I do this."

Linda nodded as she sealed a box of candy to be mailed out. "I don't think I'll ever get tired of it. I won't get tired of eating it either." She chuckled.

"You and me both," Carrie said. They were both working on filling the online orders that had come in overnight. I was glad that we had great employees here at the candy store. There was rarely an issue among us, and I realized now that was nothing short of a miracle. It had been a while since I had worked at another job, and the time I had spent at the jewelry store made me even more grateful for what I had.

I glanced at the clock. "I don't know if any of you are tired of donuts, but I think I have enough time to get us some before we open if anyone is interested."

"I would love a donut," Carrie said.

Linda nodded. "I'm always ready for a donut."

"And iced coffee?" Mom asked, turning to me. She had been working double time making fudge this morning. We had been selling out of it every day, and this was the last weekend of Pumpkin Hollow Days, so the pumpkin spice fudge was going to go like hotcakes. Or like fudge. Because who doesn't like fudge?

"I'll hurry back." I set the tray of fudge on the rack with all the others so it could cool, picked up the skirt of my Cinderella costume, and hurried out front. "I'm going to get donuts."

Christy turned to me. "I'm going to go with you. Everything is done out here." She ran back to let Mom know, and we headed out. It was still forty-five minutes until opening, so the small crowd that waited out front of the door each day wasn't there yet. If we hurried to get the donuts and coffee, we could be back before the crowds formed.

"Pumpkin Hollow Days has gone by so fast. I haven't had any time to take in any of the attractions," she said, holding up the skirt of her Rapunzel costume. Her braided wig was tucking into the waist of her skirt while she worked this morning.

I nodded. "Me either. Working at the Jewelry store took up a lot of time. But I told Ethan I intended to take a hayride either tonight or tomorrow night."

"That sounds like fun. The carousel broke down. Did you hear that?"

I looked at her. "No. When did that happen?"

She shrugged as we walked along. "A customer told me yesterday that it was closed and had been for the entire Pumpkin Hollow Days. I didn't even notice."

"Huh. It hasn't been that long ago that Sam Connor refurbished it and got it running again."

"It's so old that I bet it takes a lot to keep it running."

I nodded. "I'll bet."

We walked in silence for a minute, then Christy glanced at me. "Mia, are you angry about what Nina said to you?"

I looked at her, then shook my head. "No. Nina just lost her husband. I'm trying to be understanding. If that had happened to Ethan, would I behave in a way that wasn't like me? I think I would."

"Yeah. Me too."

There was a small line at the bakery, and I inhaled as we stood in it. It smelled so good in here. If I wasn't making candy, I might like to work in a bakery. How could you ever get tired of the scents that hung in the air?

After a few minutes, we made our way to the front counter. Angela had an employee helping her, and that made the line move along. She smiled at me and Christy.

"Hello, girls. It's hard to believe that Pumpkin Hollow Days is almost over, isn't it?"

"We were just talking about that on the walk over here," I said. "It went too fast, but at least there's the Halloween season coming up."

She nodded. "I can hardly wait. What can I get you? A dozen donuts?"

I smiled and nodded. "And five iced vanilla lattes. It's going to be a busy day, and we will need the caffeine."

"Can I get six of those sugar cookies?" Christy asked. "They always look so good, and I've got to have some."

"No problem."

She got to work on the drinks first, and the bell over the door rang as it opened. Christy and I turned to see who came in, and it was Joe Feldman. I turned away. After the last encounter I had with him, I didn't want anything to do with him.

He got in line behind us. "What are you doing in here?"

I glanced over my shoulder and was surprised to see that he was talking to me. "What?"

He looked at me. He was wearing another dirty blue chambray shirt and jeans that were too loose on him. In his hands he held a tattered black wallet, and he was looking through it, his fingers moving too fast. "You. What are you doing here? I've got some coins I need to sell to you."

I frowned. "Joe, I don't work at the jewelry store. I work at the candy store."

"You were there the last time I was there. I don't want you to cheat me like you did before."

Angela was looking at me. I sighed and turned back to Joe. "I was only filling in over there. I work at the candy store. You've seen me there plenty of times." I thought I could smell alcohol from where I stood.

He snorted. "Filling in? I don't believe that. If you work at the candy store, why would you be at the jewelry store?"

I glanced at Christy, then turned back. "Because Nina Black's husband was murdered, and she needed some time off to be with her family. I was doing her a favor."

He chuckled, a rough, grumbly sound. "Poor old George, shot dead right in his own store. Ain't that a kick in the pants?"

"It's a lot more than a kick in the pants," Christy said. "It's awful, and it's a crime that someone is going to have to pay for."

He snorted. "That George was a thief. Stole money from me every time I brought something in there to sell. He deserved what he got."

"What kind of donuts would you girls like?" Angela asked.

I turned to look at her, and her eyes were wide, trying to communicate something to me.

"Just an assortment is fine," I said.

Christy turned around. "George didn't get what he deserved. Some horrible person murdered him in cold blood. No one deserves that."

Joe laughed. "Some people deserve so much more than that. George deserved what he got. He was a thief, and you can't spend your life going around cheating people, because it will catch up to you, eventually. And it did."

"Mia, I have two boo-berry donuts if you'd like them. I know they're your favorite."

I nodded absently and turned back to look at Joe.

Christy was just getting heated up. "That's ridiculous, and you know it. Maybe it was you who was ripping George off with junk jewelry?"

Angela shook her head at me. "Christy, did you want to pick out the sugar cookies? The ones with the pumpkin patch are cute." She turned to her open kitchen door. "Mary, there's a customer. Can you come out and give me a hand?"

"You don't know what you're talking about," Joe said to Christy. "I only brought him heirlooms that my grandparents left me. He was a thief!" Joe's face had turned red, and I could sense that he was about to blow.

"Mary, why don't you help this gentleman?" Angela said, nodding toward Joe.

Mary was young and probably just out of high school. She smiled and hurried to the counter. "What can I get for you, sir?"

Joe glared at us but scooted over. "I need two dozen donuts, and I don't want just anything thrown in there, either. You'll pick the little ones. I'll tell you what I want."

I looked at Angela, and she shook her head, then leaned over the low counter. "Be careful with that one. Once he loses his temper, he gets really ugly."

I nodded. "I've seen him in action."

"What a jerk," Christy mustered, peering into the display case. "Those pumpkin patch cookies are cute. Give me three of those and three of the haunted house ones, please."

"Has he blown up in here?" I asked Angela while she finished our order.

She nodded. "He ran into someone he didn't like in here once, and he lost his temper. I was afraid someone was going to get hurt. I almost called the police, but a squad car pulled up and parked in front. He settled right down, then."

"I bet he did," Christy said.

I glanced down at the end of the counter. Joe wasn't a nice person, and obviously didn't care about George being murdered.

Chapter Nineteen

I SIGHED, LOOKING OVER the empty candy store. It was Monday morning after Pumpkin Hollow Days had ended and we were finally getting a breather. The shop was still decorated for Halloween and would stay that way through the end of the year, although some of the decorations would be replaced with a few Thanksgiving decorations and a lot of Christmas ones. But all of the Halloween decorations were never put away. Some stayed all year long. Ethan and I never did get our hayride, but that was fine because the hayrides were going to continue through the rest of summer, and it would be less crowded now anyway.

Mom came out of the kitchen with a tray of chocolate fudge with walnuts, the pumpkin spice having been put on hold until the Halloween season began. According to Mom, it isn't special unless it's kept for special occasions. She smiled when she saw me standing there. "What are you doing, Mia?"

I shrugged. "Just looking around. I love the new decorations you bought this year. I saw these cute little pumpkins online that

I think will look good in the corners of the shelves. They had a vintage feel to them, and you know how I love vintage."

She nodded, opening the back of the display case. "I certainly do. They sound cute. I've deemed Pumpkin Hollow Days a success, but I am ready for a short break."

"Me too." I went to lean on the counter. The Monday after Pumpkin Hollow Days ended was usually quiet, as if everyone needed a rest. The tourists stayed home, and the townspeople slept in. It was nice.

"Has Ethan had a break in the case yet?" She closed the display case door.

I shook my head. "Not yet. He's a little down, but these things take time."

She nodded. "Of course they do."

I looked at her. "I've been thinking. I hate how things ended with Nina. Do you think I should go talk to her? See if she still thinks I stole that bracelet? I hate leaving things undone, and right now it feels very undone."

Her brow furrowed. "I don't know. I haven't spoken to her since she stopped by the candy store. I'm doing my best not to feel put out with her, but I'm afraid that I do. But at the same time, I can understand how she feels. Maybe we should give it a few more days and see how we feel about it then?"

I nodded. "That's probably best. I think I'm going to stop by Amanda's and get a coffee. Would you like one?"

She nodded. "I can't pass that up. How about a gargoyle's poison?"

"Wow, you need the caffeine, don't you?"

She chuckled. "If I plan to stand on my feet all day, I do. It may be quiet in here, but we've got a lot of online orders that need to be filled."

Linda came out of the kitchen with a tray of bonbons. "It feels good to be out of costume today. No matter how much fun it is to dress up, I'm always more comfortable in a t-shirt and athletic shoes."

"Me too," Mom said.

"I'm making a coffee run to Amanda's, Linda. What would you like?"

"How about a jack-o'-lantern? Hot?"

"That sounds good. I think I may have to have one, too. I'll be right back."

The gargoyle's poison had a triple shot of espresso along with maple and cinnamon, and the jack-o'-lantern was a pumpkin spice latte with white chocolate. Amanda was great at making up new flavors of coffee, and although it was still technically summer, I was done with it. Fall was my favorite time of year, and it couldn't come soon enough.

I waved at Polly as she swept the sidewalk in front of the gift shop. "It's a beautiful morning!" she called.

I nodded. "It sure is!"

I had to pass the jewelry store on my way to the Little Coffee Shop of Horrors, and I slowed my pace. Mom was probably right. I should wait a few days before trying to talk to Nina. There was still the possibility that she had killed George, but I had a hard time believing it. Or at least, I didn't want to believe it. I stopped and looked in the window. There were some cute tennis bracelets with orange, yellow, green, and amber stones in them. They were probably not genuine gemstones, but they were cute anyway. I still didn't know what happened to the diamond tennis bracelet, and I hoped Nina had come to her senses and understood that I would never steal from her. Or anyone else.

As I stood there, I wondered how much of a disaster it would be if I went to talk to her now. Elizabeth's car was parked near the corner of the street, and I frowned just thinking about her. There was something that was not right about her, in a big way. Then there was Joe Feldman. No one doubted he was off. Had he killed George? I thought it was possible. We hadn't heard anything from Grace since she had been fired, although I was getting an enormous number of hang-ups from a blocked number, and I was pretty sure I knew who was behind it. Ethan had talked to her after she stormed out of the candy store, so maybe that kept her from doing more than calling and hanging up on me. I thought she was a very real suspect as well. And then we had Elizabeth. Something was going on her with her that I couldn't put my finger on. Her control tactics were evidence of something more sinister, I was sure.

Sighing, I pushed the door open, the little bell announcing my arrival. But the sales floor was empty. I stopped. Maybe Elizabeth was working by herself. I realized I hadn't seen Nina's car out front, and I started backing up. There was no reason to stick around if it was only Elizabeth working.

A muffled sound came from the back room, and I could have sworn it was the word help. I froze. Something else was said, but it too was muffled, and I told myself to get out of there, but my feet wouldn't move.

Elizabeth appeared in the backroom doorway, smiling with her best customer-service smile. But when she saw it was me, she glared. "What do you want? Nina doesn't want you in this shop. You're a thief and a liar. Get out!"

I stood there, frozen in place. "Where's Nina?" I managed to squeak out.

"She's at home, trying to grieve for her poor, dear, dead husband. You and your family made a terrible mess of things. I told her not to let you come in here, that no good could come of it. You've stressed her out so bad that she has to take an extra week off. Now, get out!"

I took a deep breath. "I heard someone say help a moment ago. It was Nina. What have you done to her?"

She shook her head, making a face that said I was crazy. "What are you talking about? She isn't here. Her car isn't out front. Now get out!"

My head started to spin. Was I hearing things? She was right that her car wasn't outside. But was she lying? I shook my head. "I want to talk to Nina."

She rolled her eyes and huffed. "Will you just get out of here? She's probably at home trying to recuperate from all the stress you've caused her."

"I didn't cause her any stress. It was you. You blamed the missing bracelet on me because you didn't want me around. Admit it. You're the liar and the thief." I suddenly understood what was going on. Elizabeth knew that I didn't take the bracelet. She did so she could set me up and get me out of here.

She looked at me, tilting her head. "Get out, or I'm calling the police. I'm sure your husband wouldn't want to be embarrassed by you getting arrested. That would be hard to take."

"Go ahead. Call the police." I didn't know if she would accept my challenge and call them or not, but I was sure that I heard Nina back there. And if she needed help, I was going to make sure she got it.

Her face went red, and she gripped her hands into fists at her side. "You're going to be sorry." She strode across the room toward me, and I dashed to the backroom.

"You can't go back there! Get out!"

There was a long display case between us, and it gave me a few seconds while she moved around it. I hoped it was enough.

When I got to the backroom, I screamed. Nina was gagged and tied up in a chair, her eyes pleading with me. Before I could turn around, Elizabeth shoved me into the backroom. I tripped but managed to stay on my feet, and I grabbed the broom, turning around to use the handle as a weapon. I struck Elizabeth in the side of the head. She screamed and grabbed her head, but the blow wasn't hard enough to knock her down, so I hit her again. That was when I saw the gun on the desk, and I lunged for it. Elizabeth screamed.

Chapter Twenty

"AH, THIS IS THE LIFE," Christy said as she snuggled next to Devon on the lawn chairs.

"You're telling me," he said. "We should do this more often. How come we don't do this more often?" He turned to look at her.

"Because we're dumb."

They both laughed. My sister was in love.

I turned to Ethan. We were sitting on our own lawn chairs, looking up into a clear, crisp summer night sky. There was a full moon and a million stars out. Nights like this didn't come along often enough. Our little cottage had a small yard in the back and in June Ethan had set up a firepit, and I was glad he had.

"I hate what she did," I said.

He nodded. "Me too. But I'm glad she didn't kill anyone else."

Elizabeth had hit Nina with the butt of the gun and tied her up, unsure of what she was going to do with her. The rumors about Elizabeth having a thing for George had been true. She had fantasized that she and George were going to get married, but George had rebuffed her each time she had tried to make a move on him. I was right that he wasn't the sort of man who would cheat on his wife.

I nodded. "I can't believe she would kill him, and then still work for Nina as if nothing had happened."

Ethan turned to me. "She said she didn't know what to do after she killed him. She wanted to leave town, but she knew we would question that and come looking for her. In the end, she decided it was safer to hide right under our noses."

"I'm not sorry she's going to jail," Christy said. "She was awful to work with. So controlling. She deserves a nice long sentence for killing George."

"I bet that control issue is what made her kill George to begin with," Devon said.

Ethan nodded and put another marshmallow on his skewer, placing it over the fire. "I believe so. She was determined to have George, and she was going to have him no matter what it took."

"That also explains why he unlocked the door for her that morning. She was an employee, and he wouldn't have questioned her showing up even though she wasn't scheduled to work." I yawned and stretched. Today had been a difficult day. My preference was to stay home and read and enjoy some snacks. Crime fighting was too strenuous and scary. Not that that would stop me from doing it, of course.

Ethan looked at me. "Next time your instincts tell you not to do something, can you follow them?"

I shook my head. "No. Nina would be dead by now if I had." Nina had decided to walk to work instead of drive, and that was why I didn't see her car. The morning had been cool and sunny, and she said she had been inside for too long and needed some exercise.

He nodded. "You're right. Maybe just give me a call first then."

"So, she couldn't have George, and she killed him," Christy said, examining her marshmallow for doneness. "Why did she tie Nina up?"

"Nina kept talking about George's death and who could have killed him. It worried Elizabeth that she knew something, and she decided she needed to get rid of her. Only, finding her body shot in the backroom of the jewelry store wasn't going to be something that would point me away from her, it would make me look at her more closely. She planned to kill her at her house, but as you may have noticed, Elizabeth had some anger issues and she lost control that morning, and she hit her. She didn't know what to do with her, and she didn't want her calling the police, so she tied her up until she could figure out what her next move would be. Mia interrupted her while she was trying to figure that out."

"Yay, Mia," Christy said. "But you really need to take me with you when you do things like that. I missed the whole thing."

I chuckled. I really didn't like when things took a turn as they had, but there wasn't much I could do about it. I was just glad that we both made it out alive.

I put another marshmallow on a skewer and held it over the fire. I was tired and ready to go to bed, but it really was a beautiful night, and we were enjoying hanging out. Why ruin it?

"Did Elizabeth steal the bracelet?" Christy asked.

"She said she never stole anything. I don't know. In the scheme of things, I'm not worried about it. We got our killer and that's what matters," Ethan said. He put his hand on mine and squeezed it. "Stay out of trouble."

"I'll try," I said, turning the marshmallow to brown on all sides. I was glad that Elizabeth had been caught before she killed Nina. It may have been Grace that stole the bracelet, or it could have been Elizabeth. It's not like I was going to believe anything she said. She was a killer, after all.

I hadn't had a chance to talk to Nina, so I still didn't know how she felt about me. Maybe after she had some time to recuperate and pull herself together after this scare, she would speak to me. Or maybe I would go and speak to her. Who knows? Saving her life probably put her in a better frame of mind where I was concerned, so I wasn't going to worry.

I scooted my chair closer to Ethan and laid my head on his shoulder. It was a lovely night to just be happy, and I decided that I would be.

The End

Books by Kathleen Suzette:

A Rainey Daye Cozy Mystery Series
Clam Chowder and a Murder
A Rainey Daye Cozy Mystery, book 1
A Short Stack and a Murder
A Rainey Daye Cozy Mystery, book 2
Cherry Pie and a Murder
A Rainey Daye Cozy Mystery, book 3
Barbecue and a Murder
A Rainey Daye Cozy Mystery, book 4
Birthday Cake and a Murder
A Rainey Daye Cozy Mystery, book 5
Hot Cider and a Murder
A Rainey Daye Cozy Mystery, book 6
Roast Turkey and a Murder
A Rainey Daye Cozy Mystery, book 7
Gingerbread and a Murder
A Rainey Daye Cozy Mystery, book 8
Fish Fry and a Murder
A Rainey Daye Cozy Mystery, book 9
Cupcakes and a Murder

Silenced Santa
A Freshly Baked Cozy Mystery, book 16
New Year, New Murder
A Freshly Baked Cozy Mystery, book 17
Murder Supreme
A Freshly Baked Cozy Mystery, book 18
Peach of a Murder
A Freshly Baked Cozy Mystery, book 19
Sweet Tea and Terror
A Freshly Baked Cozy Mystery, book 20
A Cookie's Creamery Mystery
Ice Cream, You Scream
A Cookie's Creamery Mystery
Murder with a Cherry on Top
A Cookie's Creamery Mystery
Murderous 4th of July
A Cookie's Creamery Mystery
Murder at the Shore
A Cookie's Creamery Mystery
A Lemon Creek Mystery
Murder at the Ranch
A Lemon Creek Mystery, book 1
The Art of Murder
A Lemon Creek Mystery, book 2
Body on the Boat
A Lemon Creek Mystery, book 3

A Home Economics Mystery Series
Appliqued to Death
A Home Economics Mystery, book 1